RA D0785679 S

Little Book *of*

RUNIC
WISDOM

For Jeanne Elizabeth Blum

RALPH H. BLUM'S
Little Book *of*
RUNIC
WISDOM

CONNECTIONS
BOOK PUBLISHING

A Connections Edition
This edition published in Great Britain in 2001 by
Connections Book Publishing Limited
St Chad's House, 148 King's Cross Road, London WC1X 9DH

British Library Cataloguing-in-Publication data available on request.

ISBN 1-85906-065-X

10 9 8 7 6 5 4 3 2 1

Please Note
Although every effort has been made to credit sources, this book may lack some
references. Any authors, or their representatives, will happily be credited as
soon as they are heard from or located.

Phototypeset in Arrus and Gill Sans using QuarkXPress on Apple Macintosh
Printed in Spain by Grafo, S.A. Industrias Graficas

Contents

Introduction

Every culture worth its salt has possessed some form of oracular tradition, some way of revealing the will of the gods to the people. An ancient Germanic and Norse alphabet, the Runes were first used by shamans and tribal leaders all across Europe. Derived from rock carvings dating from the Second Bronze Age (circa 1300 B.C.E.), and similar in function to the Greek Oracles and to the *I Ching* (the Chinese "Book of Changes"), the Runes were last in general use in Iceland during the late Middle Ages.

In their contemporary form, the main purpose of the Runes is to help us determine what is right action in any given situation. My own work with the

Runes began in the late 1970s. On countless occasions since then, the Oracle has proven a strong teacher and wise guide.

The quotations offered in this volume are drawn largely from my books: *The Book of Runes* through *The Healing Runes,* and *Relationships—A Compass for Conduct.* Because there are three different sets of Rune interpretations, you will find the same Rune appearing under different names. For example, Rune 8 can be Fertility, Intimacy, or Faith. I have also included quotations dating from antiquity to the present, words that have illuminated my path, as I hope they will illuminate yours. Where no source is indicated, you may assume that the words are mine.

This small book has two functions. First, it is a "Book of Days"—365 daily readings with one extra for leap years. Originally, a Book of Days was designed to inform and educate, and sometimes ran to several volumes. In this work it is my intention to support the reader by providing a useful meditation for each day.

The second function is to serve as an oracular resource. At challenging moments, when a stressful situation is pressing on your mind or unsettling your heart, open this book at random to find clarity or guidance. After assembling the first draft of this manuscript, I made such random readings part of my own practice. Almost invariably, the passage to which I turned proved to be pertinent, thought provoking, or reassuring.

Occasionally, when I am consulting *The Book of Runes*, and drawing a single Rune is not enough, I pick again. In my experience, the message of this second Rune, added to that of the first, always provides the clarity I need. The same appears to hold true for this work.

It is my hope that this *Little Book of Runic Wisdom* will prove to be a welcome companion on your journey.

Gud blessi thig and Aloha.

Ralph H. Blum   HAIKU, HAWAII

May the Runes
serve you as a compass
for conduct

January 1

DAY
1

You to whom all hearts are open, all secrets known, hear our prayers ... With nothing in our hands to which we cling, with listening minds and lifted hearts, we pray ... We ask that prayer be second nature to us now, deeper than a habit, the very heartbriar of our lives ... Above all, we pray for the precious care of our souls ... We pray, and our prayers turn to praise upon our lips.

—*The Healing Runes*, Rune 16, Prayer

The world stands out on either side
No wider than the heart is wide.
And overhead is stretched the sky
No higher than the soul is high.
Something can push the sea and land
Further apart on either hand.
But he whose soul is pinched and dry,
The sky will crush him by and by.

DAY
2

—Edna St. Vincent Millay, *Renaissance*

DAY
3

I want to learn to work with the undeveloped aspects of myself, areas of stunted growth, weaknesses I project onto others. I am put on notice that I can accept setbacks all along my path until I understand the source of my suffering.

—*The Book of Runes*

hat is an Oracle? Remember Delphi?
The woman sitting on a tripod,
breathing fumes out of the earth,
advising an Athenian general: "If you march
tonight, a great kingdom will fall." The oracular
justified in Psalm 38: "Be still and know that I am
God." As well as the advice to listen within by
Pinocchio's pal, Jiminy Cricket: "Always let your
conscience be your guide." And then there's the
outstanding definition offered by James Coburn,
Buddhist, drummer, actor, who called the Runes "a
compass for conduct." Anyway, that's the idea.

DAY
5

While thinking about what the Runes really provide us with, I found this: "At certain times in our lives it is comforting to have immediate access to information about our overall well-being, our physical, mental, emotional, and spiritual health that is not available through regular channels." A special fitness report, so to speak, from an expert—the expert being you.

—Notes for *RunePlay*

The journey is toward self-healing, self-change
and union. You are concerned here with nothing
less than unobstructed, perfect union. And yet
the union of Heaven and Earth cannot be forced.
Regulate any excesses in your life. Material
advantages must not weigh heavily on this journey
of the self toward the Self. Stand apart even from
like-minded others. This part of the journey—the
soul's journey—cannot be shared.

DAY
6

—*The RuneCards*, Rune 20, *Raido*, Journey

DAY
7

It's high time someone treated the Runes as part of living Western shamanism. We need our shamans, after all. And besides, you don't need an appointment to see your Runes.

—Margaret Mead, conversation in 1982

The greatest remedy for anger is delay.

—Fortune cookie, Soho, London, 1968

DAY
9

No less than sitting meditation, the way of the oracular individual entails a practice as venerable as the sacred texts of any spiritual tradition … There is a new breeze tugging at the tattered banners of the oracular, a feeling that deeper wisdom is available to each of us, if only we can access its blessings.

—Notes for *The RuneCards*

R emember that you are consulting an Oracle ...
An Oracle does not give you instruction as to
what to do next, nor does it predict future
events. An Oracle points your attention towards those
hidden fears and motivations that will shape your
future by their unfelt presence within each present
moment. Once seen and recognized, these elements
become absorbed into the realm of choice. Oracles do
not absolve you of your responsibility for selecting
your future, but rather direct your attention towards
those inner choices that may be the most important
elements in determining that future.

—Dr. Martin D. Rayner, preface to *The Book of Runes*

Do not look for answers where at the moment no answers can be given. Live through it. Live your questions. Live. And maybe sometimes, without knowing, you will live into the answers.

—Rainer Maria Rilke

The winter of the spiritual life is upon you. You may find yourself entangled in a situation to whose implications you are, in effect, blind. You may feel powerless to do anything except submit, surrender, even sacrifice some long-cherished desire. Be patient, for this is the period of gestation that precedes a rebirth.

DAY
12

—*The Book of Runes*, Rune 23, *Isa*, Standstill

I remember John Gray standing against the
Maui night, his arms lifted up in supplication,
his eyes tight shut, praying this simple prayer:

DAY
13

> *Healing Energy,*
> *I need your help.*
> *Come to me now.*
> *Thank you.*

Speak these words aloud to begin or end your
day or at any moment that calls for healing.

Living an Oracular Life is my attempt to
identify the pattern in what I am already
doing and subject the choices I make to an
oracular measure. As I write, the songlines
make themselves known, genetic memory
uncoils and rises until its hooded eyes stare
into my own. I want to be in the places
where that happens. I want more than
almost anything else to have a true present.

DAY
14

—*Living an Oracular Life*

DAY
15

It was Martin Luther King Jr. who said, "Whatever affects one directly affects all indirectly." If I really meditated upon those words, and if I really acted as if they applied to me and to all I think and say and do, my world would change. And indirectly, so would yours. No doubt about that.

With wisdom comes the knowledge that the only person I can change is me.

—Robert Lee O'Hare

Oracle, from the Latin *oraculum*, divine announcement … 1. among the ancient Greeks and Romans, a) the place where, or medium by which, deities were consulted; b) the revelation or response of a medium or priest; 2. a) any person or agency believed to be in communication with a deity; b) any person of great knowledge or wisdom; c) opinions or statements of any such oracle; 3. the holy of holies of the ancient Jewish Temple.

—*Webster's New World Dictionary*

Events or, more likely, aspects of character can interfere with the growth of new life. You may feel dismay at failing to take right action. And yet rather than dismay, what is called for here is diligence. Perhaps you will be required to cultivate the soil once again, for through correct preparation, growth is assured.

—*The Book of Runes*, Rune 16, *Berkana* Reversed, Growth

What I remember best

Was that the door

To your room

Was the door to mine.

—Ann Sexton

Taking offense is as violent as giving offense.

—Michael Beckwith, Minister, Agape Church, Los Angeles

The oracular is simply the occasion for bringing into play an omen. The burning bush was an omen to Moses; all omens speak, that's their job. And yet they relate to inner hearing before they have anything to do with seeing.

—Dr. Allan W. Anderson

What is to give light
must endure burning.

DAY
22

—Viktor Frankl, author, psychiatrist, Holocaust survivor

When did you last feel listened to in such a way that you knew the other person really got where you were coming from, really understood your motives, concerns, and fears? When did you last listen to someone in such a way that they knew, without a doubt, that they had been heard and acknowledged?

DAY
23

—*Relationships—A Compass for Conduct*

So we must agree to accept the things we cannot change, and there is a blessing in that. Because while we may not manage to alter the present situation, what we can do is change our response to that situation. That's our freedom, a freedom that will, in time, permit us to move on. And it can take work. And persistence. And boldness. And courage. And several varieties of fortitude. Still, who ever said it was easy to exit this labyrinth, this maze?

DAY
24

—Notes for *The Serenity Runes*

DAY
25

Secrets are the enemies of Intimacy.
As is being "too busy" all the time.
Find a moment in the midst of the
day's occupations to share your tender
thoughts and good feelings with your
partner. Intimacy is the lubricant for
relationship, and it is most effective
when it takes the form of shared
humor and laughter.

—*Relationships—A Compass for Conduct*, Rune 8, *Inguz*, Intimacy

ooking around, I make a real-time inventory of Divine Presence the way my teacher, Wanda Gale, taught me. I imbue and charge everything I see or touch with God's presence in this manner, saying:

God is with me. God is in the air I breathe, God is in the breeze, God is in the gears of my truck, God is in the gravel of our drive, God is in the pond, God is in the water hyacinths, God is in my fingers, God is in the keys of my PowerBook ... God is with me, God is with me, God is with me ...

And I continue to do so until I feel surrounded by God, immersed in God.

This is a life-enhancing practice. Use your own words. Do it often.

Each morning I say my prayers and sit for ten minutes, conscious of my breath. Then I draw a Rune to gain added insight regarding what God has in mind for me this day. And sometimes, at day's end, when life has been particularly challenging or rewarding, I go to the Runes again for a grade, an indication of how I used my life this day.

Honor your passage into darkness.
Honor the dying.
The new life holds promises
   unimagined by the old.

DAY
28

—*The RuneCards*, Rune 5, *Uruz*, Strength

DAY
29
Pain is the craft entering into the apprentice.

—Medieval French

F ree of anxiety, willing to be radically alone
and unattached to any outcome, the Spiritual
Warrior practices absolute trust in the struggle
for awareness, and is constantly mindful that what
matters most in life is to have a true present. For
where else can power be applied? The power to
change, the power to love oneself, one's God, one's
neighbor and all sentient beings. A true present.
May I see the hands of those who have managed
to make a mistake in the future?

DAY
30

There really is no secret to living an oracular life.

—Notes for *The Book of Runes*

My God is a God of long isosceles triangles: Seeds planted decades ago burst into flower in my life now. For instance, when we needed the money for a down payment on our Maui home, it came from a young man whose grandfather in South Africa in 1892 bought a mule that found its way to the diggings that became the Kimberley diamond mines. That magical mule transported the down payment across a hundred years.

DAY
31

God, make the door of this house wide enough to receive all who need human love and friendship, yet narrow enough to shut out all envy, pride and strife. Make its threshold smooth enough to be no stumbling block to children nor to straying feet, but rugged and strong enough to turn back the tempter's power. God, make this house a gateway to your eternal kingdom.

AMEN

—Woman's house prayer, Anonymous

DAY
32

DAY
33

The Runes are an instrument for learning the will of the Divine in our lives, a means of listening to that part of ourselves that knows everything we need to know for our lives now. As a method of guidance and self-counseling, the Runes assist us to navigate unfamiliar waters when the old charts no longer serve and we are required to be our own cartographers … first and foremost, the Runes are a training device for strengthening the intuition which is, I suggest, everybody's second language.

—*The Book of Runes*

February 3, 1997. Jeanne and I have lost
a child. A Maui woman said, "Well, it's only
the end of the first trimester." But I say,
"You came, Child, to practice a touch-and-
go landing." And so I have made this verse
for you:

> *Winter flower,*
> *such a brief stay*
> *how little we knew*
> *Of your fragrance.*

DAY
35

Whether one believes in a religion or not, and whether one believes in rebirth or not, there isn't anyone who doesn't appreciate kindness and compassion.

—Tong Tinh Thong's office wall, London

I had forgotten that the Greek meaning for the word "incubation" was originally to sleep within the precincts of a temple in order to receive a vision, or revelation, relief from disease or pain, or to encounter a god. What do you need to incubate in your life? What problem are you willing to give over to sleep? Ask for divine help as your head settles on the pillow.

DAY
36

The sacred mirror of truth now lies
in front of you. Pick it up in silence
and, without fear, look into your
present situation. Ask if you are
being honest, first with yourself, and
then with others. To be honest with
oneself is where all healing begins.

—*The Healing Runes*, Rune 11, Honesty

Long ago, I set out to compose a
simple prayer directed to the Divine
that was unqualified by name or form.
It took me over a year. What I finally
came up with was a prayer of only six
words, and they are these:

I will to will thy will.

Hey, John Denver, the first time we met, while we were still shaking hands, you grinned and said, "I've used your Runes for a long time. They're a great support system. So thanks."

I was too tongue-tied to tell you how long I've been nourished by your music. Well, better late than never. So thanks …

Sing on, John, sing to us in your sun-steeped voice from beyond the bridge of swords.

There's no such thing
as unbelief.
It's just a matter of what
you believe in.

DAY
40

—John Robert Stevens

Please don't bully me about
meditation. Weeding in the garden
can be a meditation. And so can
washing your car. I have found that
making your own Runes can be a
profound and satisfying meditation.
As can drawing a Rune from the bag.

—Notes for *The Book of Runes*

In prayer,
come empty,
do nothing.

—St. John of the Cross

DAY
43

Love is the language in which
God speaks. For when we listen
with love, it is the heart that
hears. Take this Rune as a simple
reminder to listen—to your
heart, to those you love, and to
the still small voice that always
speaks for love.

—*The Healing Runes*, Rune 6, Love

By aligning ourselves with the will of God and praying specifically, we can become co-creators in the course of events. God himself is involved in the general direction of things, but forming the specific intentions is the very work that we're called to do as we pray.

DAY
44

—Matthew Fox and Rupert Sheldrake, *Natural Grace*

DAY
45

Take these words and stand them like so many glowing candles in the forests of the night. Listen, and I will speak to you about serenity.

—*The Serenity Runes*

The idea of relationship needs to fall apart. When we realize that life is the expression of death and death is the expression of life, that continuity cannot exist without discontinuity, then there is no longer any need to cling to one and fear the other. There is no longer any ground for the brave or the cowardly. One sees that relationship is the lack of any viewpoint whatsoever.

DAY
46

—Chögyam Trungpa, *The Heart of the Buddha*

If you believe little else, believe this, and repeat it aloud until it sticks and sinks in: I am the authority for all that I do.

—Akshara Noor, *Modest Mantras and Sensible Sayings*

Now is not a time to seek credit for accomplishments or to focus on results. Instead, be content to do your task for the task's sake. Herein lies the secret of experiencing a *true present*.

DAY
48

—*The Book of Runes*, Rune 1, *Mannaz*, The Self

Sitting on a boulder, in the spring sunshine, we were talking about our lives, and Elissa said to me: "In a few weeks I get my degree. I won't be a student anymore. I'll open my own practice. And I'm moving out. And I'm getting married." Then she looked at me, smiled, and said, "In fact, I'm changing all my stories." What a refreshing moment. What a useful insight. How often do any of us change all our stories?

Laguz supports your desire to immerse yourself in the experience of living without having to evaluate or understand. It speaks to the satisfaction of emotional needs, to the awakening of the intuitive or lunar side of your nature. For while the sun strives for differentiation, the moon draws us toward union and merging.

DAY
50

—*The Book of Runes*, Rune 18, *Laguz*, Flow

Here is a thought so simple that it might seem trivial, and yet it lies at the heart of acceptance: Where you are now is just fine, because that's where you are, and you have a perfect right to be there. Anyone who is

DAY
51

reluctant to support you in being where you are, at this moment, is no friend of acceptance.

There is a special kind of valor in accepting the truth of what is happening in our lives ... for until we can grasp the power of acceptance, there is no possibility for lasting change.

—*The Healing Runes*, Rune 14, Acceptance

Sum up at night what thou hast done by day,
And in the morning what thou hast to do.
Dress and undress thy soul: mark the decay
And growth of it: if with thy watch, that too
Be down, then wind up both: since we shall be
Most surely judged, make thy accounts agree.

DAY
52

—George Spencer

DAY
53

Find a bell whose sound you like. Then, two or three times, at random moments throughout the day, let it be sounded. And when you hear the bell, cease all activity. No talking, no working on whatever you were doing. Still your mind, simply sit or stand quietly and breathe. Just for a minute. Then let the bell sound again.

This bell meditation or calling a time-out, serves as a circuit breaker in our daily rounds, to bring us back to our center, where peace is our true activity.

How can the random selection of marked
stones tell you anything about yourself?
Perhaps these Rune interpretations are
simply so evocative that each contains
some point which can be accepted as
relevant to *some* part of what is happening
at the limits of consciousness any day,
any time, to anyone.

DAY
54

—Dr. Martin D. Rayner, preface to *The Book of Runes*

DAY
55

It may seem too simple, but when I feel stuck, unable to find the clarity to take the next step, I hear my mom's voice saying, "This too shall pass."

—Notes for *A Yoga of Gratitude*

News of Berne Clark's death reached me when I was in rural Japan. He was the first of my generation to die. I could never tell when my sadness would capture me. Yet I was comforted by the Rune of Grief: "Know that even the deepest grief, when fully felt, will lessen and soften over time. There is a calm to be found on the far side of grief, a peace unknown to those who have yet to grieve." In the deep of winter. I wrote:

DAY
56

> *Flowering plum branches*
> *in a street vendor's arms.*
> *O how I miss you.*

Examine your limitations: You come from a certain background, you have lived your life in a particular way. As your limitations become clearer to you, you will begin to see that various notions you hold about yourself are not supported by the reality of your life … Through this process of limiting and specifying, your view of yourself will become clearer and more simple.

—*The RuneCards*

Any occasion of conflict between you and
your partner is an opportunity to come to
terms with your limitations. Since it is so easy
to find fault with one's partner, make a
commitment to avoid the Four Cs: Criticizing,
Complaining, Condemning, and Comparing.
Deleting these four nasty habits from your
arsenal will completely transform your
relationship.

DAY
58

—*Relationships—A Compass for Conduct*, Rune 7, *Nauthiz*, Limitations

DAY
59

Of the divine oracles, some are spoken by God himself with his prophet as interpreter, some were revealed through question and answer, others by Moses himself, when inspired and possessed and transported out of himself.

—Philo of Alexandria

Follow the glistening dew drops
 to the center of the web.
Limitations define us,
Ordeals temper us.
See the Great Teacher
 behind every disguise.

—*The RuneCards*, Rune 7, *Nauthiz*, Constraint

March 1

DAY
6 1

Pain passes,
but beauty remains.

—Auguste Renoir

When my life feels most unmanageable,
when the past becomes a litany of blame
and guilt and the future a storm front of
fear, the Serenity Prayer buoys me up with
its quiet common sense.

DAY
62

> *God grant me the serenity*
> *to accept the things I cannot change,*
> *the courage to change the things I can,*
> *and the wisdom to know the difference.*

—Introduction to *The Serenity Runes*

Peace of mind is clearly an internal matter. It must begin with your own thoughts and then extend outward. It is from your peace of mind that a peaceful perception of the world arises.

DAY
63

—*A Course in Miracles*

O You whose ways are our ways when we let them be,
Hear our prayer.
Provide us with a set of sacred tools,
Whose right use can be lovingly detected in each
    other's eyes,
Tools that loose their benediction on our ancient bondage,
And heal us from all wounds of separation,
Tools that, in our hands, define us as your children.
And so we offer up the fruit of this our prayer.
Help us, we pray, to bring it forth
From the highest possible place
And for the greatest possible good.
AMEN

DAY
64

—*Relationships—A Compass for Conduct,* Invocation

DAY
65

Fire is Heaven's light
in its palest hue.
That fiery branch
burning at the heart's center
claims its kinship
with the sun.
What hid itself in shadows
is clear to me now.

—*The RuneCards*, Rune 14, *Kano*, Opening

Patterns of Recognition help us identify rarely sighted creatures of habit hiding in dense bush, creatures that will sometimes reveal themselves to us once they become aware that we can both hear and comprehend what they have to say for themselves. To describe them, we require what Kenneth Burke called "a grammar of motives."

DAY
66

If it is time to turn your relationship into a life partnership, there are two affirmations that can only work for good, only support and protect your intention. They are these: *I am committed to telling you the truth, and, I am committed to keeping my agreements.*

—Notes for *Relationships—A Compass for Conduct*

*Knowing that what is mine will
   come to me,
I release the old and give thanks for
   the blessings
of my life. I am ready and willing
   to embrace change.*

DAY
68

—*Relationships—A Compass for Conduct*, Rune 18, *Laguz*, Change

Often when I feel in need of divine encouragement, I recite my favorite road prayer: *Maranatha*, a single word in Aramaic whose meaning is, "Come Lord."

Ma-ra-na-tha. The tradition from which it descends is deep and ancient, steeped in the practice of sages and teachers and saints, a fine tradition of meditation. I subscribe to that. And although I often go months without saying it, I always come back to it: *Maranatha … Come Lord!*

So simple and elegant and powerful.

Visualize yourself standing before a gateway on a hilltop. Your entire life lies out behind you and below. Before you step through the gateway, pause and review the past: the learning and the joys, the victories and the sorrows, in truth, everything it took to bring you here. Observe it all, bless it all, release it all. For it is in letting go of the past that you reclaim your power.

Step through the gateway now.

—*The Book of Runes*, Rune 21, *Thurisaz*, The Gateway

DAY 71

Trust yourself, my dear. You know more than you think you do.

—Dr. Benjamin Spock to Cynthia Childs

Remember this: That there are
entities that support and encourage
and sustain us in our effort to live in
harmony and engage in right action.
Call them what you will—Angels,
Guides, Helpers—they are generous,
they are free of all limitations, and
they are with us always.

DAY
72

—Notes for *Living an Oracular Life*

DAY
73

The Practice of Council is simple. The basic rule is this: Speak from the heart, listen with the heart. Nobody ever interrupts anybody. A "talking stick" (any object you favor) helps, since the one holding the stick speaks until they are done, and only then does the stick pass. Useful in relationships, family, business, any community situation, Council is always applicable whenever two or more are gathered together.

Bestow, O god, this grace upon us:
That in the school of suffering
we should learn self-conquest, and
through sorrow, even if it be
against our will, learn self-control.
AMEN

—Aeschylus (525–456 B.C.E.)

Good fortune and bad fortune are not predestined; we bring them on ourselves by our conduct. And all of the consequences of good and evil follow as the shadow follows the body.

—Kan Ying Phien

You have prepared the ground and planted the seed. Now you must cultivate with care. To those whose labor has a long season, a long coming to term, *Jera* offers encouragement of success. Know that the outcome is in the keeping of Providence and continue to persevere.

DAY
76

—*The Book of Runes*, Rune 13, *Jera*, Harvest

DAY
77

The task is to define oneself, *for* oneself, in a manner that enables a relationship *to* oneself. In so doing, one becomes who one truly is.

—Dr. Allan W. Anderson, in conversation

*Hear Odin now: It is better not
  to offer than to offer too much,
  for a gift demands a gift,
Better not to slay than to slay
  too many.
Thus did Odin speak before the
  earth began
when he rose up in after time.*

DAY
78

—*The Poetic Edda* (c. 1200 C.E.)

In seed time learn, in harvest time teach,
*   in winter enjoy.*
The road to excess leads to the palace
*   of wisdom.*

He who has suffered you to impose on him
*   knows you.*
The bird a nest, the spider a web,
*   man friendship.*
Eternity is in love with the productions
*   of time.*

—William Blake, *Proverbs of Hell*

B e in the world but not of it. And yet do not be closed, narrow, or judging; rather, remain receptive to impulses flowing from the Divine within and without. Strive to live the ordinary life in a non-ordinary way. Remember at all times what is coming to be and passing away, and focus on that which abides. Nothing less is called for from you now.

DAY
80

—*The Book of Runes*, Rune 1, *Mannaz*, The Self

DAY
81

And still the waters rise.
  Crossing the deeps,
a messenger brings
the promise of new life unfolding.
  Oh Ancient of Days,
may the beauty of your intention
  show in our faces.

—*The RuneCards*, Rune 3, *Ansuz*, Signals

On a hot summer day, with a tide of tourists coursing through St. Patrick's Cathedral in New York, I asked a grizzled priest, a man built like a trash compactor, if it was permissible for an Episcopalian to take Communion. He growled: "Do you believe in the Presence?" Without hesitation, I said, "I do," and he said, "Then you're welcome to take Communion." And he turned on his heel and left me standing there.

It was the only question that needed answering.

DAY
82

Stealing anything from anyone is a confession that you do not trust the Divine as your Supply Sergeant.

This Rune is a flare that illuminates the field where lovers meet and passion is the prize. Receiving *Teiwaz* is an invitation to allow yourself intensity of feeling in all your endeavors. Enthusiasm, the gift of love-making, a reverence for life itself, your relationship with the Divine—all this is deserving of your passion. And it is in our passion for each other that we will find a reflection of God's passion for us.

DAY
84

—*Relationships—A Compass for Conduct*, Rune 15, *Teiwaz*, Passion

Whatever the cause of your suffering, and whatever the reason for your pain, make certain that you cause no pain and no suffering, to another. The former is part of all coming to be and passing away; the latter is bad karma and bad manners and makes no sense.

DAY

85

—*Thoughts of a Buddhist Lover*

Socrates, who the oracle of Delphi called the wisest of humans, relied on oracular communications to guide him in daily life … But when asked to explain what oracles were and where they came from, the philosopher declined. He would only call them "divine somethings."

—Dianne Skafte, *Listening to the Oracle*

DAY
87

The starting point is the self.
Its essence is water. Only
clarity, willingness to change, is
effective now. For from correct
relationship to yourself comes a
right relationship to all others
and to the Divine.

—*The Book of Runes*, Rune 1, *Mannaz*, The Self

If you can't find the strength to change your attitude, write down ten things for which you are truly grateful. I am always amazed at just how quickly this simple exercise improves my state of mind. And my attitude.

DAY
88

On a book tour, back in the early 1980s, in a motel on the outskirts of St. Joseph, Missouri, I found these words written in flash red lipstick on the glass mirror above the bureau:

Are the mountains to the West, Jacob? It's so hot and the child's trying to live, but dying trying. Please, Jacob, find our home ...

Across the years, each time I remember them, those words cause me to picture a young pioneer family in its travail, and each time I feel a deep ache in my heart.

Every successful relationship makes a music all its own, separate melodic themes that blend smoothly in two-part harmony. There is pleasure to be found in talking intimately, making plans and dreaming together, even in being silent together, or saying out loud, "I'm glad you're in my life." When two people share common values, experiences and interests, even defeats can be dealt with in a good way.

—*Relationships—A Compass for Conduct*, Rune 20, *Raido*, Harmony

DAY
90

Some people have black belts in complaining. A lot is happening in my life, some of it quite intense, some of it painful and severe. Yet surveying it all, I am unable to see that I have any insurmountable problems, so I have no reason to complain.

We have only to remember: In the life of the spirit, we are always at the beginning. Remembering this helps us to overcome our addiction to "getting ahead." For when we experience a true present, that is where everything happens.

DAY
92

—*The Book of Runes*

There is no need for temples;
no need for complicated philosophy.

DAY
93

Our own brain, our own heart is
our temple; the philosophy
is kindness.

—The 14th Dalai Lama

What is called for here is to consider your issue with care and awareness. First disperse resistance, then accomplish the work. For this to happen, your will must be clear and controlled, your motives correct. Any dark corners should be cleansed; this must be carried out diligently and sometimes with expert help. Modesty, patience, fairness and generosity are called for here. Once resistance is dispersed, and rectification carried out and seen to hold firm, then through steadfastness and right attitude, the blossoming can occur.

DAY
94

—*The Book of Runes*, Rune 16, *Berkana*, Growth

I am the guide who has been guiding me. I am the voice I have been hearing. This shift in identity causes a major and complete reversal of energy.

—Letter from Barbara Marx Hubbard

The darkness is behind you, daylight has come. Nevertheless, you are reminded not to collapse yourself into thoughts for the future or behave recklessly in your new situation. Considerable hard work can be involved in a time of transformation. Undertake to do it joyfully.

—*The Book of Runes*, Rune 22, *Dagaz*, Breakthrough

A butterfly emerges
still moist from the cocoon.
DAY
97 *This is how new life comes,*
softly, secretly,
among the green shoots.

—*The RuneCards*, Rune 8, *Inguz*, Fertility

As surely as your way is distinct from
my way,
there is in all matters also a third way.
To find it, let us pass together through
the gates of compromise.

—*Relationships—A Compass for Conduct*, Rune 21, *Thurisaz*, Compromise

DAY
99

Resentment is worse than acid and bile. It has been said that to cling to resentment is to harbor a thief in your heart. For resentment robs you of your energy, your strength, your peace of mind and, ultimately, your ability to heal.

—Notes for *The Healing Runes*

Love thy neighbor as thyself …
Why does this commandment
cause us so much difficulty?
Perhaps the problem lies
in assuming that we actually do
love ourselves. Was that easier
to do in biblical times?

Jeremiah said that the Tables of the Law are written on the heart. He wasn't concerned about what was written on stone.

My grandfather regarded burning
candles as landing strips for angels.
As a child, I used to pass hours
picturing a multitude of celestial
beings dropping down out of the
darkness for a fiery landing.

Some say that passion wanes over the years. When we are fortunate, however, passion evolves and grows as we grow, attaching itself to the Relationship as a condition and a blessing.

—*Relationships—A Compass for Conduct*, Rune 15, *Teiwaz*, Passion

Home means leaving, coming back, losing it, remembering, and having had one once, so we know it is neither magic nor beyond the horizon of possible imagining. And sometimes home means you are loved and accepted and forgiven.

From the Tao, as from the Greek Oracle at Delphi, we hear the identical teaching: "Know thyself." Among the coordinates of effective healing, the power of those two words has no equal.

—Notes for *The Healing Runes*

R emember the burning bush and the voice in the whirlwind? Well, the Runes are the home version: user-friendly, with an infinite data base and totally democratic in nature. As for their timeliness, remember that function determines form, use confers meaning, and an Oracle always responds to the requirements of the time in which it is consulted—and to the needs of those consulting it.

DAY
107

The Oracle reminds us that we were not born to live in pain, but rather to transform our lives through a greater understanding of ourselves and the world around us ... If you are still avoiding the truth of your situation, take this opportunity to remember that it requires hard work, time, and understanding, to come out of denial, out of hiding.

—*The Healing Runes*, Rune 9, Denial

Oh what am I that I should have the best of everything! Now, that's low self-esteem, isn't it? But at least you can jump up from there. If you're young and ignorant and know nobody, you're in a good place, aren't you? There's plenty of space above you, after all.

—From a conversation with John Michell

Seeking after wholeness is the Spiritual Warrior's quest. And yet what you are striving to become in actuality is what, by nature, you already are. Become conscious of your essence and bring it into form, express it in a creative way. A Rune of great power, making life force available to you, *Sowelu* marks a time for regeneration down to the cellular level.

—*The Book of Runes*, Rune 24, *Sowelu*, Wholeness

Let go of all worry, Beloved, for
all you are doing is serving God.
And whatever the vow is, take it
afresh each day. Say to the Divine: DAY **110**
"This is your day. I am going to live
it for you."

—Notes for *The Healing Runes*

DAY
111

Our lives are ordered for us by the Divine so that nothing is too much. We are never given more than we can handle; but nothing is too loose, either. We can always breathe, yes, but at times the water is up to where the wings of the nose barely touch. And as we grow? As we grow, the water rises. Still we are preserved from drowning. And that is providential, because our nature needs a situation that reminds it: You are always at the beginning. In the life of the Spirit, you are always at the beginning.

—Dr. Allan W. Anderson

Courage is the art of being the only one who knows you're scared to death.

—Earl Wilson, *The Hollywood Reporter*, June 11, 1947

Sit in silence and observe your breathing. As you breathe, think these words:

> (on the in-breath) *Breathing in, I calm body and mind.*

> (on the out-breath) *Breathing out, I smile.*

After a while, change the phrase to:

> (on the in-breath) *Dwelling in the present moment.*

> (on the out-breath) *Wonderful moment, only moment.*

A minute or two will suffice to ready you to consult the Oracle. Or for anything life presents.

—*The RuneCards*

The ways of love are often
hidden and secret. Yet once
initiated into love's ways, they
become our ways. And when
that happens, love is everywhere.

—*The Healing Runes*, Rune 6, Love

You can disagree with someone
and still treat them with respect.
And where there is mutual
respect, love can grow, regardless
of circumstances, preferences or
differing beliefs.

—*Relationships—A Compass for Conduct*, Rune 9, *Eihwaz*, Respect

Feed your faith and you will be deeply nourished; feed your doubts, and they will starve you.

—Akshara Noor

DAY
117

Well, Runa died this morning in my arms. I have run away from three dying people in my life, so I had to go through it—just be with her, let her go on her own. And thanks to her, I've lost my fear of death, from being there for her, and she picked the time.

—Bronwyn Jones, on the death of her cat, Runa

"To teach is to learn twice," said Joseph Joubert. This strikes me as a tidy amplification of *A Course in Miracles*, where it says, "We are all teachers, and what we teach is what we need to learn, and so we teach it over and over again until we learn it." Which in turn is an upgrade of "If at first you don't succeed, try, try again."

DAY
118

Remember the old story about the farmer who was so eager to assist his crops that he went out at night and tugged on the new shoots? There is no way to push the river; equally you cannot hasten the harvest. Be mindful that patience is essential for the recognition of your own process which, in its season, leads to the harvest of the self.

—*The Book of Runes*, Rune 13, *Jera*, Harvest

You can live alone or you can coexist with one another. There is a progression: to respect, to affirm, to empower, to interact for the common good. It is always a good choice.

—Alan B. Slifka, conversation

"Why was I born?" In other words, what is Heaven's mandate for me?

According to my teacher, Dr. Alan W. Anderson, "In addressing this question, you are preparing to discover what is missing in your makeup that you are here to acquire—patience, strength in the face of adversity, or any other underdeveloped aspect of the self, the acquiring of which will enable you to navigate your ideal passage through this life."

Pick a Rune for that one when you're ready.

—Notes for *The Book of Runes*

DAY
121

A SMALL PRAYER

*Teach me what I need to know
and show me where I need to go.*

*Give me the patience, the alertness,
the courage and the enduring heart
to follow that guidance and that path.*

We are responsible for our presence in the world. We have choices to make, that's what morality is about. We either make them or fail to make them. Even failing to make choices is a moral decision. Choices create our morality and our distinctness.

—Matthew Fox and Rupert Sheldrake, *Natural Grace*

Listen, I am persuaded that God desires His Will to be made known to creation. To do so is to honor the light. I am convinced that Divine Will *is* discernible, and that the map God reveals to us supports our stand in the present and our walk in the future.

—Preface to *The RuneCards*, Rev. Wallace K. Reid

As Brugh Joy reminds us in his useful guidebook, *Joy's Way: A Map for the Transitional Journey*, there are three sets of mental fetters to give up if you want to be truly free: judging, comparing and needing to know why.

—*The Book of Runes*

I think continually of those
  who were truly great …
Born of the sun, they travelled
  a short while toward the sun
And left the vivid air signed
  with their honor.

DAY
126

—Stephen Spender, *I think continually …*

DAY
127

Serenity serves us in so
many ways. Honesty leads to
serenity and patience issues
from it. Grief, anger and fear
are resolved in its embrace.
Then too, trust and faith are
nourished by serenity, and love
thrives in its presence.

—Notes for *The Healing Runes*

Ask to receive instruction or
healing—whatever it is you
need—during the night, while
you sleep. Often, what you
yearn for will come to you in
the form of a dream.

—*RunePlay*

Some things there are in life we cannot do alone, and while they are few, these few form ridge poles … And yet, as two together, we encompass far more than life yields to the solitary traveler.

Bless me with awareness
of beauty, and the skills
to share it with you.

DAY
130

Why would you worry over much in choosing whom you shall marry? Choose whom you may, in time you will find you have got somebody else.

—John Hay

Consider the constant cycling of death and rebirth, the endless going and return. Everything you experience has a beginning, a middle and an end, and is followed by a new beginning. Therefore do not draw back from the passage into darkness: When in deep water, become a diver.

—*The Book of Runes*, Rune 5, *Uruz*, Strength

If you really want to examine a situation in depth, use the Five Rune Spread. The elements involved are these:

1. An overview of the situation.

2. The challenge inherent in that situation.

3. The course of action called for.

4. What you must give up or sacrifice.

5. Some sense of the new situation that is evolving as a result of the action you take.

—Notes for *The Book of Runes*

*Lift up the self by the Self
And don't let the self droop down,
For the Self is the self's only friend
And the self is the Self's only foe.*

DAY
134

—*Bhagavad Gita*, Chapter 6, Verse 5

Here are some "Do's":

- Do begin each day with a promise to respect others
- Do sit down and talk quietly
- Do listen carefully to what others say
- Do look for things to appreciate in others
- Do give praise out loud for the good you see in others
- Do tell others they are worthwhile and important to you
- Do speak in a quiet voice even when you disagree
- Do pass up chances to insult, attack, or criticize
- Do take responsibility for life, and let others do the same

—The New York County Alternative Assistance Program

Here are some "Don'ts":

- Don't look for things to criticize
- Don't make fun of or laugh at others
- Don't tell others how to run their lives
- Don't ignore or insult others
- Don't put people down in front of others
- Don't say others are bad, or you wish they were dead
- Don't call others names like fat, ugly, stupid, or worthless

—The New York County Alternative Assistance Program

DAY
137

Respect requires the careful and conscious setting of boundaries. When we have respect for ourselves, we naturally respect our partners and honor their boundaries. Boundaries can be viewed as safe and useful meeting places where we can learn about our differences without demanding that the other person change.

—*Relationships—A Compass for Conduct*, Rune 9, *Eihwaz*, Respect

It's not really enough to know you're treading on someone's toes. It's really important to get off.

—Susan Blum, aged 13, Eliot House Dining Hall, 1953

If you cannot change
the people around you,
change the people
you're around.

—Anonymous

Unconditional love thrives in the absence of resentment and guilt, for then there is nothing to stand in its path. Yet how will you give that kind of love to another if you cannot feel it first for yourself? There is nothing "selfish" about self-love. It is simply what God asks of us with the command to *love thy neighbor as thyself*. As we learn to love ourselves, we also grow in our ability to give and receive love.

DAY
140

—*Relationships—A Compass for Conduct*, Rune 1, *Mannaz*, Loving Kindness

Lately, I've been making it my practice to listen a lot. So when someone is talking to me, I keep my mind focused on them—their voice, their words, their message. I don't interrupt, think how I'll respond, or let myself be distracted by critical thoughts. I've noticed that people are really grateful to be listened to attentively, without interruption.

Nothing external matters
here, except as it shows
you its inner reflection.

—*The Book of Runes*, Rune 6, *Perth*, Initiation

WATER RUNES
Step One:
I cleanse myself of all selfishness,
resentment,
critical feelings for my fellow beings,
self-condemnation
and misinterpretation of my life experiences.
Step Two:
I bathe myself in generosity,
appreciation,
praise and gratitude for my fellow beings,
self-acceptance
and enlightened understanding of my life experiences.

—Notes for *The Book of Runes*

Be aware of what you do, of
what you think, of what you
project. Learn to become
consciously aware of everything
you put into motion at all times.

—Winged Wolf, *Recognizing God*

People used to say, "He behaves like he was being chased by demons." Now, just because we don't say such things much anymore doesn't mean that demons are an extinct or even an endangered species. Most demons have something in common. At first, a demon is very attractive, seductive even. Then it keeps you awake at night, and soon it starts souring your life.

Resentment is a demon. A computer can be, too. And don't leave out "that old demon, rum."

Check your life for demon prints or spoor.

Be particularly attentive to personal relationships.
At this time, ruptures are more likely than
reconciliations and effort may be required to
keep your good humor. Whatever happens, how
you respond is up to you. The requirements of
your process may totally disrupt what you had
intended. Desired outcomes may elude you. And
yet what you regard as detours, inconveniences,
disruptions, blockages and even failures and
deaths will actually be rerouting opportunities,
with union and reunion as the only abiding
destinations.

DAY
146

—*The Book of Runes,* Rune 20, *Raido*, Movement

I know no better posture for entering into prayer than this one from *A Course in Miracles*: "With nothing in our hands to which we cling, with lifted minds and listening hearts, we pray."

Runes and charms are very practical formulae designed to produce definite results, such as getting a cow out of a bog.

—T. S. Eliot, *The Muse of Poetry*

Being supportive is a natural part of our
nature. Knowing you have someone in your
corner who cares about you is always a
blessing. This Rune urges you to strengthen
your ability to endure hardship in order to
achieve a good outcome under pressure.
When you support your partner—praising,
encouraging, letting them know you are there
for them—you both grow stronger, and the
Relationship prospers.

DAY
149

—*Relationships—A Compass for Conduct*, Rune 15, *Teiwaz*, Passion

You can hear the Word, you can read the Word, and you can copiously quote the Word. But if you don't live the Word, then all else is in vain, a yawn.

Here is what Queen Elizabeth I is reported to have said when asked for her opinion of the Holy Sacrament:

> *'Twas God, the Word, that spake it.*
> *He took the bread and brake it.*
> *And what the Word did make it,*
> *That I believe, and take it.*

The plow of change invariably cuts across the furrows of our settled lives. What changes are called for now in your relationship? Is there a need for deeper intimacy? For fewer expectations? For greater awareness of when you are being judgmental? Receiving *Laguz*, consider what it is you are being asked to change so that the relationship may grow. The ability to open to change is an essential part of the yoga of relationship.

—*Relationships—A Compass for Conduct*, Rune 18, *Laguz*, Change

The meditation bell sounds.
Body, speech and mind
In perfect oneness
I send my heart along
With the sound of the bell

May the hearer awake
From forgetfulness
And overcome anxiety and sorrow.

—Thich Nhat Hanh, *Ojai Foundation Workshop*

June 1

The term of travail is ended and you have come to yourself in some regard. The shift that was due has occurred; now you can freely receive *Wunjo's* blessings, whether they be in material gain, in your emotional life or in a heightened sense of your own well-being. This is an alchemical moment in which understanding is transmuted from knowledge. The knowledge itself was a necessary but not sufficient condition; now you can rejoice, having been carried across the gap by the will of Heaven.

—*The Book of Runes*, Rune 12, *Wunjo*, Joy

WAYS OF SEEING

The real voyage of discovery consists not in seeking new landscapes but in having new eyes.

—Marcel Proust

Lord, grant me weak eyes for things that are of no account and strong eyes for all thy truth.

—Søren Kierkegaard

We walk by faith and not by sight.

—St. Paul

JUNE 3

When I speak,
    I speak from my heart.
When you speak,
    I listen with my heart.

DAY
155

—*Relationships—A Compass for Conduct*, Rune 3, *Ansuz*, Communication

166

I beseech the immaculate Master of
*   Monks to steer my journeys;*
May the Lord of the lofty heavens
*   hold His strong arm over me.*

This is thought to be the oldest surviving
Christian verse-prayer in Icelandic;
composed by a Hebridean poet during the
colonizing voyage of Eirik the Red from
Iceland to Greenland, possibly in the
summer of 985 or 986 C.E.

Impulses must be tempered by thought for correct procedure. *Do not attempt to go beyond where you have not yet begun.* Be still, collect yourself, and wait on the Will of Heaven.

DAY
157

—*The Book of Runes*, Rune 21, *Thurisaz*, Gateway

Inscription on the Ruthwell Cross,
Dumfriesshire, Scotland, 900 C.E.:

> *krist waes on rodi*
> *hwethrae athear fusae férran kwomu*
> *aththilae til anum ic theat bih(eald)*
>
> *Christ was already on the Cross*
> *Still many came swiftly, journeying from afar,*
> *Hurrying to the Prince. I beheld it all.*

The poem's author is unknown. The "speaker"
in the poem is the wood of the Cross, telling
what it was like to hold our crucified Lord.

DAY
159

ach time you draw *Wunjo*, regardless of the challenge you may be facing, take it as an invitation to celebrate what is pleasing and nourishing in your life. Find the good and praise it. Celebrate your victories, the hardships you have overcome, a job well done. Celebrate the family and friends who care about you and would miss you if you were not in their lives. Connect with all the blessings you enjoy.

—*Relationships—A Compass for Conduct*, Rune 12, *Wunjo*, Celebration

Although I find myself saying it often, it bears repeating: the Runes provide guidance and you determine the answer. To give someone an answer, my grandfather was fond of saying, robs them forever of acquiring that answer for themselves.

—Notes for the *Mechanism of the Oracle*

We are living in an age of radical
discontinuity. The lessons come
faster and faster as our souls and the
universe push us into new growth …
The old maps are outdated;
we require new navigational aids.
And the inescapable fact is: *You are
your own cartographer now*.

—*The Book of Runes*

Spiritual power comes into your experience when you
understand the true meaning of prayer. As a person,
you have no spiritual power of your own. You are but
the transparency, the instrument through which the
power of God flows to the world and to the people of
the world.

DAY
162

—Joel S. Goldsmith, *The Altitude of Prayer*

Now, I have no interest in argument, yet it is difficult
for me to pass that statement by *sans* calling to mind
friends who seem to radiate a soft and subtle power
of their own. And yet, Joel Goldsmith well might ask,
where are the boundaries between Earth and Heaven?

173

DAY
163

Let no thought, action, belief
cause you to imagine that you are
separate from one or more of your
fellow humans, since we all are
God's and separating from one
another is, by definition,
separating ourselves from Him.
This one takes practice.

What do we mean when we speak of "family values"? Simple traditional virtues: Loyalty, stability, taking responsibility for your life and earning your way, speaking honestly, loving God as we understand God, singing together the old familiar hymns. These are core values and they are much the same the world over.

DAY
164

—*Relationships—A Compass for Conduct*, Rune 4, *Othila*, Home and Family

DAY
165

Consider the meaning of profit and gain in your life. Look with care to know whether it is wealth and possessions you require for your well-being, or rather self-rule and the growth of a will.

—*The Book of Runes*, Rune 11, *Fehu*, Possessions

People are often unreasonable, illogical, and
self-centered. Forgive them anyway.
If you are kind, people may accuse you of
selfish, ulterior motives. Be kind anyway.
If you are honest and frank, people may
cheat you. Be honest and frank anyway.
The good you do today, people will often
forget tomorrow. Do good anyway.

DAY
166

—Mother Teresa, internet wisdom

Feeling lonely? bored?
depressed? angry?
Well here's a fine
remedy: It's called
making an immediate
difference in someone
else's life.

The hallmarks of respect are courtesy and kindness. Whatever the situation confronting you, be mindful that the ways in which you express your truth— tone, feeling, attitude—are as telling as the facts themselves. Facts are always open to interpretation, while the courtesy and the kindness with which you express your position speak for themselves.

DAY
168

—*Relationships—A Compass for Comfort*, Rune 9, *Eihwaz*, Respect

DAY
169

Enjoy your good fortune and
remember to share it: The
mark of the well-nourished
self is the ability and
willingness to nourish others.

—*The Book of Runes*, Rune 11, *Fehu*, Possessions

To realize an idea, you must first set your intention. Goals are simply dreams to which you've added a deadline.

DAY
170

I asked the postal clerk for a receipt for my package, and she said that I was at the wrong window if I needed a receipt. So I said, "O well, I'll just trust the Lord to get it there safe." And she said (STAMP! STAMP!), "I trust Him for all of mine." And I said, "For all your what?" And she said, looking up at me, "All of my help." (STAMP! STAMP!) "Without him I can't do nothing anyway." (STAMP!) "The good, the bad, all of it. That'll be two dollars."

—Dolores, of Lennox Hill P.O., New York City

You are reminded that
you must first draw from
the well to nourish and
give to yourself. Then
there will be more than
enough to nourish others.

—*The Book of Runes*, Rune 3, *Ansuz*, Signals

Yes, there are things to give up. And yes, by all means, undertake change. Yet rather than think of it as something heavy, like sacrifice or renunciation, think of it as the fine tuning—or better yet, the editing—of your desires.

I know why we bless
our food: We bless our
food because we want
God to be in it.

DAY
174

DAY
175

Let your mind be easy about intimacy—you were born for it. It is everywhere love is: sharing simple chores, drinking from the same cup, understanding without explaining. It is the same thought coming to you both in the same instant. True intimacy will mark you as together, even if you are separated halfway around the world. That is the grace of relationship. That is heaven on earth.

—*Relationships—A Compass for Conduct*, Rune 8, *Inguz*, Intimacy

When you're on overload, just
remember that you have the skills and
the spiritual depth to handle it. Find
quiet time; write down what's the most
important issue, then handle it first. In
the Secret Service we had a saying,
"Absence of evidence is not evidence of
absence." That is, you can't do much
about much hypothetical uncertainty.

DAY
176

—Jerry Parr, head of Presidential Protection the day Mr. Reagan was shot

DAY
177

Destiny, as used here, means your ideal passage through this life, your ideal possibility ... At the same time, Destiny means confinement, for your Destiny is realized as the direct result of life's limitations.

—*The Book of Runes*

Control of the emotions is at issue here. During times of transition, shifts in life course and accelerated self-change, it is important not to collapse yourself into your emotions, the highs as well as the lows.

—*The Book of Runes*, Rune 10, *Algiz*, Protection

DAY
179

There are fundamental laws
through which Spirit operates
in our lives, and one of them is
this: *Where right action is
concerned, we are never coerced.
We are always free to resist.*

—*Relationships—A Compass for Conduct,* Rune 16, *Berkana,* Right Action

Friends of mine get together when a young man needs to "undergo rites." They take him out into the northern California woods and tell him good things to do and bad ones he must never do: Never hit a woman. Listen to the old people. Yes, there's a God, but God's a mystery; let's leave it at that. There's things you can ponder but there's a limit. Remember that you're a man, so sit down and think before you act.

Campfires, drumming, and fasting are optional but useful.

Perseverance and foresight are called for here. The ability to foresee consequences before you act is a mark of the profound person. Avert anticipated difficulties through right action, this Rune is saying. Yet even more than we are *doers*, we are *deciders*. Once the decision is clear, the doing becomes effortless, for then the universe supports and empowers our action.

—*The Book of Runes*, Rune 9, *Eihwaz*, Defense

Anger is only one letter
short of danger …
To handle yourself,
use your head; to handle
others, use your heart …

DAY
182

—Ascribed to Eleanor Roosevelt

July 1

How often it seems that when we are at our most unlovable, we are most in need of love.

—Richard Storrs Childs

I marvel at all the ways there are of sending prayer's arrows heavenward: From those who say, "Lord, in your mercy, hear our prayer," to William Butler Yeats, grown old, writing,

> *"I pray, for fashion's way is out,*
> *And prayer comes round again,*
> *That I may die, though I seem old,*
> *A foolish passionate man."*

To Sister Wendy who, when Charlie Rose asked her on television what she asked for during her four hours of daily prayer, replied, "O Charlie, I don't ask. I listen."

For everything that
lives is holy.
Life delights in life.

—William Blake

There's something to be said for bowing. Not necessarily going all the way, prostrating oneself, banging heads on cobbles, the old "kowtowing." But making a physical recognition, yes. Bowing to the mother and father that gave us birth (GONG!). To the grandparents (GONG!). Bowing in gratitude to the teachers who taught us to understand how to die in the present moment (GONG!). In gratitude to our friends, those on our path who gave us support (GONG!). In gratitude to all species and to the animal, vegetable, and mineral realms, we bow (GONG!).

DAY
186

Be careful if you meddle
in the affairs of dragons,

because from their point of
view, you are crunchy and
taste good with ketchup.

—Internet wisdom

If faith is the wick in the candle of Divine Love, let our wicks be trimmed by all that life decrees, so that we burn brightly in fair fortune or adversity, ill health or rapture, turning aside from none of it.

DAY
188

—*Relationships—A Compass for Conduct*, Rune 25, The Mystery

Let there be love shared among us.
Let there be love in our eyes.
Now let your love sweep this nation.
Cause us, O Lord, to arise.
Give us a fresh understanding,
Sharing a love that is real;
Let there be love shared among us;
Let this be love that we feel.

—Handwritten words pasted into a hymnal in a Catholic church in
East Molesey, Surrey, England

There is no such thing as a bad
Destiny, for your Destiny is the
Divine's desire for your Highest Good.
There is an energy that ceaselessly
moves us to change for good rather
than ill, and that energy is the
outworking of Divine Will in our lives.
In other words, your Destiny is your
spiritual destination.

DAY
190

—*The Book of Runes*

I see a black sail on the horizon
set under a dark cloud that hides the sun …
Bring me my Broadsword and clear understanding
Bring me my cross of gold as a talisman
Bless with a hard heart those who surround me
Bless the women and children who firm our hands
Put our backs to the North wind. Hold fast by
    the river
Sweet memories to drive us on for the Motherland.

—Jethro Tull, "Broadsword"

The dunes shift
and shift forever,
    feather grass restless
        in the wind.
Cool your emotions.
    Follow your path.
That is your protection.

—*The RuneCards*, Rune 10, *Algiz*, Protection

As a rule, anything that provides you with more options is some kind of blessing. And while it's been said before, it bears repeating: Forgiveness may not change the past, but it does enlarge the future.

The philosophy of waiting is sustained by all the oracles of the universe.

—Ralph Waldo Emerson

I saw a stranger yestereen;
I put food in the eating place,
  Drink in the drinking place,
  Music in the listening place;
And in the sacred names of the Triune
He blessed me and my house,
  My cattle and my dear ones.
And the lark said in her song:
  Often, often, often,
Goes the Christ in the stranger's guise.
  Often, often, often,
Goes the Christ in the stranger's guise.

—From the Gaelic

As the poet Milton reminds us in
On the Morning of Christ's Nativity
(1629), it happens sometimes that
"the Oracles are dumb." Well,
nothing is perfect or consistent.

Then again, perhaps such a moment
of silence is perfect and consistent;
certainly it is respectful.

Deep in the collective unconscious of humanity
—and perhaps in its very heart—lies the desire
to worship a revealing God who will disclose
to believers everything they need to know for

living a full and productive life.

And to that end, each religion has a place
for the oracular. An Oracle can be a Divine
saying and/or a vehicle for discerning Divine
Wisdom.

—Dr. Wallace K. Reid, preface to *The RuneCards*

You may see fit to withdraw or even to retreat in the face of a pressing situation, especially if events or people are demanding that you expend your energy now. Know that such a retreat is a retreat in strength, a voyage inward for centering, for balance. Timely retreat is among the skills of the Spiritual Warrior.

DAY
198

—*The Book of Runes*, Rune 24, *Sowelu*, Wholeness

Leading an authentic life has to do with being true to archetypal patterns that are expressions of the Self. When this is so, what we do has a sacred dimension and gives us a sense of meaning.

—Jean Shinoda Bolen, therapist, author

We all come into this life with a cross to bear. Perhaps it is a condition that lasts a lifetime, a pattern of adversity we must undergo in order to grow in self-awareness and self-rule. Each of us is defined by our strengths and, equally, by our limitations. The challenge is to embrace our limitations so we may enjoy a healthy relationship with ourselves, and a successful relationship with an intimate partner.

DAY **200**

—Notes for *Relationships—A Compass for Conduct*

Because the timing is right, the outcome
is assured although not, from the present
vantage point, predictable. In each life
there comes at least one moment which, if
recognized and seized, transforms the course
of that life forever. Rely, therefore, on radical
trust, even though the moment may call for
you to leap empty-handed into the void.

DAY
201

—*The Book of Runes*, Rune 22, *Dagaz*, Breakthrough

Gratitude is the highest, the most elegant form of courtesy.

—Anonymous

Be strong and of good courage; do not be afraid or dismayed, for the Lord your God is with you wherever you go.

—Joshua 1:9

What can you do to restore trust if it is absent from your life? Or to create it where it never was? I reckon trust is both sacred and ordinary—the foundation upon which we build our lives, and upon which we do God's work in the world. However painful the moment may be, this Rune urges you to have faith and know that, as you heal, you *will* be able to trust again.

—Notes for *The Healing Runes*

The warrior ship
plows the waves,
yet no hand grasps the tiller,
none draws an oar.
Oh mariner,
surrender to the mystery.
All else follows.

—*The RuneCards*, Rune 17, *Ehwaz*, Movement

Remain mindful that Runecraft is not intended as a substitute for prayer, but rather as a companion activity to the outworking of the Divine Plan for you in your life; a useful, but never necessary activity, since prayer alone is always sufficient.

—Notes for *RunePlay*

And Jesus was a sailor
When he walked upon the water
And he spent a long time watching
From his lonely wooden tower,
He said, All men shall be sailors now
Until the sea shall free them,
And he sank beneath your wisdom
  like a stone.

—Leonard Cohen, "Suzanne"

Peace, love, forgiveness, faith, hope, and joy—is
that not a world-class, timeless recipe for having
life more fully? And notice: "joy" not "happiness."
Joy is the ticket to ride. And notice, if you will:

> *Lord, make me an instrument of your peace.*
> *Where there is hatred, let me sow love.*
> *Where there is injury, pardon.*
> *Where there is doubt, faith.*
> *Where there is despair, hope.*
> *Where there is sadness, joy.*

—St. Francis of Assisi

DAY
208

The seed of God is in us ...
Pear seeds grow into pear trees,
hazel seeds into hazel trees,
and God seeds into God.

—Meister Eckhart

When the heart of relationship is full, nourishment is everywhere, even in the smallest things, for God is always found in the details.

—*Relationships—A Compass for Conduct*, Rune 13, *Jera*, Abundances

When a relationship rests on a foundation of mutual trust, there need be no barriers to intimacy. Is the trust between you whole and intact? Does it flow in both directions? Are there any places where trust has been weakened and as a result, intimacy is suffering?

—*Relationships—A Compass for Conduct,* Rune 10, *Algiz,* Mutual Trust

There is one elementary truth, the ignorance of which kills countless ideas and splendid plans: that the moment one definitely commits oneself, then providence moves too. All sorts of things occur to help one that would otherwise never have occurred. A whole stream of events issues from the decision, raising in one's favor all manner of incidents and meetings and material assistance which no person would have believed would have come their way. Whatever you think you can do or believe you can do, begin it. Action has magic, grace, and power in it.

DAY
212

—Goethe

DAY
213

As we grow more in touch with our life's purpose, we find ourselves able to manage problems with peaceful minds, meet challenges with courage, and gain confidence from every test along the way. Each breakthrough brings greater understanding, and we experience more fully the pleasures, the victories and rewards that purpose provides.

—*Relationships*—*A Compass for Conduct*, Rune 22, *Dagaz*, Purpose

1 August

In this fateful hour, I call upon all Heaven with its
*   power,*
And the sun with its brightness
And the snow with its whiteness
And the fire with all the strength it hath
And the lightning with its rapid wrath
And the winds with their swiftness along the path
And the sea with its deepness
And the rocks with their steepness
And the earth with its starkness
All these I place, by Heaven's almighty help and grace,
Between myself and the powers of darkness.

—Welsh Rune, traditional

DAY
215

When you find your way, and you know your assignment, there's nothing else to do but do it. It will give meaning to purpose. The rest is to learn relationship—with our mates, our sons and daughters, grandchildren, and with everyone who pushes our buttons. Most of all with our mates.

—Judy Whitson, midwife to *A Course in Miracles*

*Your children are not your children. They are the sons
and daughters of Life's longing for itself:
They come through you but not from you,
And though they are with you yet they belong not to you.*

DAY
216

*You may give them your love but not your thoughts,
For they have their own thoughts.
You may house their bodies but not their souls,
For their souls dwell in the house of tomorrow,
Which you cannot visit, not even in your dreams.*

—Kahlil Gibran, *The Prophet*

DAY
217

The Third Commandment exhorts us to Honor thy father and thy mother: that thy days may be long upon the land. We can take that a step further, and honor our ancestors. Honor their strengths, be aware of their weaknesses. We have genetic memory in our DNA. Are your fears and phobias their nightmares? Look to your ancestors for some light on your difficulties to understand patterns and cravings and phobias.

—Jeanne Blum

Be a lover of gateways.
Approach them softly.
For once you pass through
there will be changes
and much that you
will gladly lay aside.

—*The RuneCards*, Rune 21, *Thurisaz*, Gateway

Deep peace of the running wave to you.

Deep peace of the flowing air to you.

Deep peace of the quiet earth to you.

Deep peace of the shining stars to you.

Deep peace of the gentle night to you.

Moon and stars pour their healing light on you.

Deep peace of the Light of the World to you.

—A Gaelic blessing

There may be considerable frustration in your life if you draw *Fehu* Reversed, a wide range of dispossessions ranging from trivial to severe. You fall short in your efforts, reach out and miss; you are compelled to stand by and watch helplessly while what you've gained dwindles away. Observe what is happening. Examine these events from an open perspective and ask, "What do I need to learn from this in my life?"

DAY
220

—*The Book of Runes*, Rune 11, *Fehu* Reversed, Possessions

Someone once suggested that we treat every person we meet today as though we knew they would be dead by morning. Show them all the love and compassion and understanding you can without expecting anything in return, and your life will be changed forever.

Let the constraints of the time serve you in righting your relationship with yourself. Use this moment to bring quiet to whatever sense of confusion or sadness you may be feeling. There is nothing you can do to change what has already happened. You can only turn it over to God.

DAY
222

—*The Healing Runes*, Rune 3, Guilt

DAY
223

For many, this is a time of separating paths. The Oracle reminds us that we were not born to live in pain, but rather to transform our lives through a greater understanding of ourselves and the world around us.

—*The Healing Runes*, Rune 9, Denial

*Where is the boundary
between Earth and Heaven?
After all, it is Love
that loves through us,
is it not?*

—*The RuneCards*, Rune 24, *Sowelu*, Wholeness

DAY
225

There are so many ways to betray someone you love—by not speaking out or standing firm, by refusing to recognize the truth, by infidelities both large and small. Indeed, there are situations where reason and logic are of little help and renewal is possible only by letting go of old grievances and simply forgiving. No exceptions, no exclusions.

—*Relationships—A Compass for Conduct,* Rune 17, *Ehwaz,* Renewal

My mom, when things got difficult, would oil the turbulent waters by saying, "It'll all be the same in a hundred years." The logic used to irritate me, and yet I find myself calling upon a distilled version of the same notion, a phrase I sometimes remember to whisper to myself: "As if it matters ..." When momentary setbacks, apparent failures and losses threaten my tranquillity, I take the long-term view: "As if it matters ..."

DAY
226

The more light you have, the better
you can see what is trivial and
outmoded in your own conditioning.
In relationships, there can now be a
mutual opening up which you may
trigger and set in motion through your
awareness that the fire of understanding
is once again available to you both.

—*The Book of Runes*, Rune 14, *Kano*, Opening

DAY
227

From you I receive
To you I give
Together we share
From this we live.

—Hawaiian prayer

DAY
229

I no longer try to change outer things. They are simply a reflection ... I concentrate on my inner vision and find my outer view transformed. I find myself attuned to the grandeur of life and in unison with the perfect order of the universe.

—*Daily Word*

Since anger is often a mask for hurt, fear, or feelings of abandonment, look beneath your anger and ask yourself: Are you feeling angry because you feel no one is listening, because it seems that no one sees you or because you have no one to turn to? Has some aspect of the present situation caused fresh pain in an old wound? Whatever may be the case, welcome anger as information. Explore it, see where it is coming from, and how it prevents you from saying what you truly mean to say.

DAY
230

—*The Healing Runes*, Rune 19, Anger

DAY
231

*O Merciful God, be Thou unto me a strong
tower of defense, I humbly entreat Thee.
Give me grace to await Thy leisure, and
patiently to bear what Thou doest unto me;
nothing doubting or mistrusting Thy
goodness towards me, for Thou knowest
what is good for me better than I do.*

—Prayer said by Lady Jane Grey before her execution

DAY
232

You know, my dear, it really doesn't matter who you love, just so long as you love

—Eric George Hebborn, sculptor and master forger

If God is Love, and we are made in God's image, then it follows that Love is what we are. Hold fast then to this one truth: Love is your abiding destiny and your natural condition.

DAY
233

—Relationships—A Compass for Conduct, Rune 25, The Mystery

It has been said that faith is not belief without proof, but rather trust without reservation, and that trust, when cared for and respected, encourages the self to blossom. Trust is divine medicine.

—*The Healing Runes*, Rune 2, Trust

DAY
235

Confucius says that, of the thirty-six ways of avoiding disaster, running away is usually the best.

The truth is that life is hard and dangerous; that those who seek their own happiness do not find it; that those who are weak must suffer; that those who demand love will be disappointed; that those who are greedy will not be fed; that those who seek peace will find strife; that truth is only for the brave; that joy is only for those who do not fear to be alone; that life is only for the one who is not afraid to die.

—Joyce Cary

DAY
236

Here are four essentials for healing:

Have Faith Be absolutely certain that the outcome will be from the highest possible place, and for the greatest possible good.

Be Calm Wait with a peaceful mind for what you know, in your heart, will come to you.

Practice Patience And while you wait, do all you can to remove all barriers to love's presence, since love is the channel for healing.

Stay in the Now The only time when healing can occur is this present moment.

—*Relationships—A Compass for Conduct*, Rune 24, *Sowelu*, Healing

I honor your gods,
I drink at your well.
I bring an undefended heart
   to our meeting place.

I have no cherished outcomes.
I will not negotiate by withholding.
I am not subject to disappointment.

—*The Healing Runes*, Invocation

DAY
239

We are not held back by the love we didn't receive in the past, but by the love we're not extending in the present.

—Marianne Williamson, *A Return to Love*

My vision is born from stillness.
Coming to stillness is the gift from the
past; learning to wait until the water is
so unruffled that I can discern on its
still surface a reflection of what is
hidden in myself. And finally, through
contemplation of the Will of the
Divine for me in my life, I will know
the Source of my vision.

—*The RuneCards*

DAY
241

A counsel against expecting too much, or expecting in the ordinary way, for the old way has come to an end: You simply cannot repeat the old and not suffer. Call in your scattered energies, concentrate on your own life at this moment, your own requirements for growth. This Rune counsels you neither to focus on outcomes nor to bind yourself with the memory of past achievements. In doing so, you rob yourself of a *true present*, the only time in which self-change can be realized.

—*The Book of Runes*, Rune 6, *Perth*, Initiation

Watch busy little kids
Not going anywhere.
They're already there.

DAY
243

At our best, each of us is a channel through which divine wisdom flows, and we are sensitive to the inner guidance that provides us with the intuitive knowing we require. But life can be hard and difficult and we are not always clear. The channels that we are become blocked by fears, silted up with self-doubt. We do not always hear the still small voice that is our natural inheritance.

—*The Book of Runes*

God within me, God without,
How shall I ever be in doubt?
There is no place where I may go
And not there see God's face, not know
I am God's vision and God's ears.
So through the harvest of my years
I am the Sower and the Sown,
God's Self unfolding and God's own.

DAY
244

—*The Book of Runes*, Invocation

September 1

When despair for the world grows in me and I wake in the night at the least sound in fear of what my life and my children's lives may be, I go and lie down where the wood drake rests in his beauty on the water, and the great heron feeds. I come into the peace of wild things who do not take their lives with forethought of grief. I come into the presence of still water. And I feel above me the day-blind stars waiting with their light. For a time I rest in the grace of the world, and am free.

—Wendell Berry

DEATH POEM

Waiting are you?
Last train? Last supper?
Chance to make amends?
Oops! Too late.

DAY
247

Disruption takes many forms: A relationship fails, plans go awry, a source of supply dries up. But do not be dismayed. Whether you created the disruption, or whether it comes from an outside source, you are not without power in this situation. Your inner strength, the will you have funded until now in your life, provides support and guidance at a time when everything you've taken for granted is being challenged.

—*The Book of Runes*, Rune 19, *Hagalaz*, Disruption

Patience yields its rewards
Time brings answers
To understand is lucky

—Taoist saying

DAY 249

As a human being, part of your self-respect lies in showing up for your responsibilities, and often it is boring and painful. Even if you don't feel a good feeling, act as if you did, for perhaps the brain can re-pattern from that. Act as if you're having fun; at least then you do not rule out the possible positive aspects. And if you act "as if" really well, people will actually believe it. Maybe then you will note changes that you like, responses you appreciate. Act "as if," and you will become.

That is part of our power.

The Sacred is indivisible,
faction-free and accessible to
all those who practice the
Presence of God in their lives.

DAY
250

—*The Healing Runes*

DAY
251

From the point of Light within the mind of God
Let Light stream forth into the minds of all.
Let Light descend on Earth.

From the point of Love within the Heart of God
Let Love stream forth into the hearts of all.
May Christ return to Earth.

From the center where the Will of God is known
Let purpose guide our little wills—
The purpose which the Masters know and serve.

From the center which we call the human race
Let the Plan of Love and Light work out
And may it seal the door where evil dwells.

Let Light and Love and Power
Restore the Plan on Earth.

—Alice Bailey, *The Great Invocation*

ny transition is dangerous. It has always fascinated me how birds sing mostly at dawn and twilight, as though they're making a statement against imminent danger even as they sing a song of rejoicing. They're issuing a warning against interrupting what is important within their own territory. Twilight and dawn are times of crisis, and I think we have twilights and dawns, cyclically, within our own journey.

DAY
252

—Angel Thompson, author, astrologer

DAY
253

True partnership is achieved
only by separate and whole
beings who retain their
separateness even as they unite.
Remember to let the winds of
Heaven dance between you.

—*The Book of Runes*, Rune 2, *Gebo*, Partnership

The Second Coming is looked upon as the resolution to all our troubles. We have to redefine that. The fundamentalists give it a physical interpretation. The liberal Christians give it a psychological one. So what is the nature of the Second Coming? It's the self awakening to what one always was, is, and ever shall be. The awakening occurs in the heart. The coming is the awakening.

—Dr. Alan W. Anderson

DAY
254

DAY
255

Self-change is never coerced; we are always free to resist. And if there is one thing to bear in mind until the truth of the words eases the heart troubled by apparent failure and loss, it is this: On the journey of the spirit, the new life is always greater than the old.

—*The Book of Runes*

WHAT A BLESSING

Don't hide.

The sight of your face is a blessing.

Wherever you place your foot, there rests a blessing.

Even your shadow passing over me like a swift bird
  is a blessing.

The great Sparing has come.

Your sweet air blowing through the city, the country,

the gardens and the desert, is a blessing.

He has come with love to our door, his knock
  is a blessing.

—Rumi

When problems arise between colleagues, friends, lovers, partners ... Consider the following:

DAY
257

1. What happened?
2. How do you feel about what happened?
3. How would you do it differently next time?
4. What results would you like to see?
5. What insight have you gained from this experience?

—*The Book of Runes*

What is the particular gift this day has given me? Who have I loved, and have I dared to love them as well as I could? Have I contributed to the well-being of another, have I enhanced their sense of dignity or expanded the possibilities of their lives? Have I flown as close to the fire at the heart of the mysteries of love and knowledge as I dare? And of everything I have received, have I given anything back?

DAY
258

—Richard Thieme, *Islands in the Clickstream*

A lame person can ride a horse. The man who is without land can be a shepherd ... The one whose mind is most free from care does not need to know their fate in advance ... Cattle die, kinsmen die, I myself shall die. But there is one thing that never dies— the reputation we leave behind at death.

—*Havamal* or *The Sayings of the High One*

Commitment has two aspects
that can only work for good,
only support and protect your
relationship. They are:
Commitment to telling you the
truth, and *Commitment to keeping*
your agreements.

—*Relationships—A Compass for Conduct*, Rune 2, *Gebo*, Commitment

Five Ps that make up a rich life, in no special order, for me:

- Partner
- Purpose
- Physical well-being
- Place (a sense of being where you belong)
- Passion for the Divine

For me, these five subtend all else. Someone suggested "Pleasure," yet I say Pleasure is seasonal, and that Joy is a higher concept anyway. In each of the Five Ps, I take joy.

What do we mean by practicing right action? Simply put: *Even when nobody is looking, and there is no way anyone will ever find out what you've done, nevertheless you do what you know in your heart to be right.*

—*Relationships—A Compass for Conduct*, Rune 16, *Berkana*, Right Action

DAY
263

Sun and moon
and your own heart
speak always of that which abides.
In solitude and stillness
know that the journey
begins and ends
with the Self.

—*The RuneCards*, Rune 1, *Mannaz*, The Self

On those occasions when I fall into a black despair that will not let me loose, I take a deep breath and begin to chant, *God is with me, God is with me …* until the claws of despair begin to loosen their grip.

DAY
264

Then, when I am feeling less bleak, I will ask: *What is the lesson from this pain?* And I will draw a Rune.

**DAY
265**

No food is better for the heart than few desires.

—Mencius

Gebo, the Rune of Partnership, has no Reverse, for it signifies the gift of freedom from which flow all other gifts.

—*The Book of Runes*, Rune 2, *Gebo*, Partnership

DAY
267

Transforming inner negativity, repairing the damage of destructive emotion, transmitting the blessings of the enlightened compassionate heart and awakened mind—this skillful means of wisdom in action becomes medicine for the mind and a shield for the heart.

—Tarthang Tulku, *A Mandala of Protection*

278

Best not to be in bondage to your desires. So what is to be done to free yourself? For a start, don't think of it as giving something up, but rather as the fine tuning—or better yet, the editing—of one's desires.

DAY
269

When will we teach our children who they truly are? When will we say to each of them, "You are amazing. You are unique. In all the world, there is no other child like you. You have the capability and the strength to accomplish anything you desire. Yes, you are incredible. So when you grow up, how could you possibly harm another who, like you, is amazing, incredible and unique?"

When will we show our children this kind of love?

—Attributed to Pablo Casals, cellist

Rise and soar on wings
of renewed spirit.
What looked familiar before
will seem strange,
what seemed strange, familiar.

—*The RuneCards*, Rune 6, *Perth*, Initiation

You give but little when you give of your possessions.
It is when you give of yourself that you truly give.

DAY
271

For what are your possessions but things you
keep and guard for fear you may need them
tomorrow? ... And is not dread of thirst when your
well is full, the thirst that is unquenchable? ...

And there are those who have little and give it
all. These are the believers in life and the bounty of
life, and their coffer is never empty.

—Kahlil Gibran, *The Prophet*

A loving relationship is created
over time by the sharing of
experiences, learning to accept
the differences between you, and
the willingness to support each
other's dreams. For all this to
occur, listening and speaking from
the heart is essential.

DAY
272

—*Relationships—A Compass for Conduct*, Rune 3, *Ansuz*, Communication

Do whatever it is that pleases you, so long as it don't never hurt nobody no way.

—Annie, street person, New York City, 2000 C.E.

This Rune's symbol is the horse, and it signifies the inseparable bond between horse and rider. Bronze Age artifacts show a horse drawing the sun across the sky. *Ehwaz* is saying, you have progressed far enough to feel a measure of safety in your position. Now it is time to turn again and face the future reassured, prepared to share the good fortune that comes. The sharing is significant since it relates to the sun's power to foster life and illuminate all things with its light.

DAY
274

—*The Book of Runes*, Rune 17, *Ehwaz*, Movement

October 1

omewhere Kabir remarks that meeting prosperity, we ought not to be joyful, just as meeting misfortune, we do well not to weep. Neither misfortune nor prosperity need disturb us. So far so good. But when he suggests that what is arranged by Destiny will surely come to pass, he loses me. You are your Destiny, and I am mine. As above, so below. And I suggest that, since we can change the tapes recorded by the subconscious before we possessed the editorial power of conscious mind, surely we must be capable of changing our destiny.

The world we live in is filled with challenges, situations that are sometimes beyond our ability to control or even to influence. Plans fall through. Life disappoints us. We disappoint each other. When such is the case, how you respond is always up to you. And it is good to remember that as one door closes, another opens. At such times, the Buddhist precept of being "unattached to the outcome" is your ally.

DAY
276

—*Relationships—A Compass for Conduct*, Rune 19, *Hagalaz*, Challenges

DAY
277

As we become conscious of our participation in the immensity of consciousness, we begin to realize that each human body-mind is constructed so as to have the capacity to receive from the pulses of the universe the knowledge and the power to make the changes that can save the world.

—Jean Huston, Ph.D., Prophets' Conference, 2000 C.E.

There are no missed opportunities: You
have simply to recognize that not all
possibilities are open to you, that not
all opportunities are appropriate. If
your limitations define what you may
not do in the world, they also
challenge you to accept yourself and
get on with what is yours to achieve.

DAY
278

—*The Book of Runes*

DAY
279

Through your awareness of divine power at work in and through you, you know that new avenues of good are opening for you. You do your part by affirming the truth of and giving thanks for right opportunities.

—*The Daily Word*

Nothing produces inner turmoil more effectively than projecting our fantasies and fears onto another person. To the extent that we believe our fantasies are real, we are bound to suffer. We will be disillusioned, because reality will have its way. Which is not necessarily a bad thing. For only when we are stripped of our illusions about our partners are we finally able to see them, accept them and love them as they truly are.

DAY
280

—*Relationships—A Compass for Conduct*, Rune 19, *Hagalaz*, Challenges

DAY
281

For others, Perth is a reminder to live with an awareness of how precious each moment is. Letting go of the past—the love we didn't receive from our parents, the betrayals, the failures, the children we never had, places we never traveled to, the unfulfilled dreams— letting go enables us to fully embrace the present, to be here now, alive, refreshed and filled with gratitude.

—*Relationships—A Compass for Conduct*, Rune 6, *Perth*, Letting Go

"Let this be a teaching" is precisely the prayer that brings strength at the instant the words are being uttered. In fact, healing energy is already present in such a prayer— present in the words we speak.

As to true love
Few witnesses are found.
And all that they can tell is:
Did it last?
And were its remnants sound?

Relationship itself is a vast resource for growth, and we are resources for each other. Not only for the blessings and gifts each of us brings, but also because of our knack for pushing each other's buttons. When we are in a relationship—be it marriage, a friendship, or family—we are compelled to deal with unfinished business, areas of immaturity where growth was stunted. When your relationship hits the wall, instead of going your separate ways, are you willing to do the work it takes to realign your hearts? Each time you do, your relationship will be renewed and strengthened.

DAY
284

—*Relationships—A Compass for Conduct*, Rune 17, *Ehwaz*, Renewal

Draw the Rune in the air, as if you were cutting it into the ether. You can either whisper its name or purr it, *Thur...iii...saz*, as you're making the strokes, call it, so you're imparting vibration to the drawing. Then sit back and call it again, until its vibration enters you, until you feel it inside you. The ultimate aim is to become the Rune.

—Doug Ashcroft, shaman, *Calling in a Rune*

THE WAY OF THE WARRIOR

If you keep your spirit correct from morning until night, accustomed to the idea of death and resolved on death, thus becoming one with the way of the warrior, you can pass through life with no possibility of failure and perform your office properly.

DAY
286

—Yamamoto Tsunenori, *Hidden Leaves*, seventeenth century C.E.

DAY
287

God be in my head,
And in my understanding;

God be in my eyes,
And in my seeing;

God be in my mouth,
And in my speaking;

God be in my heart,
And in my thinking;

God be at my end,
And at my departing.

—Sarum Missal

To be free from repulsion and attraction, or from the wish to take or to avoid, to enter into a mood of complete impartiality— this is the most profound of arts.

DAY
288

—*The Tibetan Book of the Dead*

I am your beloved,
*   you are my true companion.*
We meet in the circle
*   at the rainbow's center,*
coming together
*   in wholeness.*
That is the gift of freedom.

—*The RuneCards*, Rune 2, *Gebo*, Partnership

It's much safer to go
on your own.
You're twice as careful.

—Earl Gill, Yukon trapper

DAY
291

Paths divide,
*   old skins are shed.*
How skillful the means
*   that free you*
*   to become more truly*
who you are.

—*The RuneCards*, Rune 4, *Othila*, Separation

THREE-PART FORMULA FOR SURVIVAL

First: Get still—get still and be still.

Second: Remember, everything you need you already have.

Third: Tell the absolute, microscopic truth as you know it.

—Iyanla Vanzant

DAY
293

It has been said that when we have compassion for one another, then we shall be of one mind. For in living a compassionate life, we are practicing the Presence of God in a simple and universal way.

—*The Healing Runes*, Rune 24, Compassion

ere are a few of the coordinates by which the strength of any committed relationship can be gauged: When did you last share secrets about your individual lives? What fears keep you from such open sharing? Do you believe that your happiness depends on your mate's changing? What are your shared priorities before God? Name seven things your mate does that you appreciate, big time. What is the climate of unconditional love in your marriage? What's your turn-around time for anger? Are you open to change even if it derails your cherished outcomes? And so it goes.

DAY
294

I start every day by forgiving everybody, releasing them to happiness—my family, myself, those who do not love me. Doing that, I'm cutting my ties, my attachments to ego, to those thoughts that keep me from rising. Forgiveness is the route and compassion is that wonderful place where you find yourself with God, because compassion is a life's work, but forgiveness is a daily practice.

—Rhonda Schaller, sculptor, teacher

Here, courtesy of an anonymous internet writer,
are some of the signs of inner peace: A willingness
to act from the present moment, rather than
from fears and past experiences. Loss of interest
in judging others and oneself. Loss of the ability
to worry. Joyful feelings of connectedness with
others and with nature. Frequent feelings of
appreciation and gratitude. A willingness to
allow things to unfold in their own time. The
ability to enjoy each moment.

DAY
296

—*Relationships*—*A Compass for Conduct*, Rune 14, *Kano*, Inner Peace

DAY
297

very relationship has its seasons. If the energy between you feels frozen or blocked, know that this is a time for reflection. Set yourself winter tasks: Release old habits, old ways of behaving that you have outgrown. Start with something you know puts a strain on your relationship. It could be as basic as always needing to have the last word. And remember this: habits that may have saved your life as a child can sabotage a mature relationship.

—*Relationships—A Compass for Conduct*, Rune 23, *Isa*, Reflection

Yesterday is history.
Tomorrow a mystery.
Today is a gift.
That's why it's called "the present!"

So live and savor every moment
This is not a dress rehearsal!

—Flotsam on the electronic tide

Great Spirit, Help us to accept the truth about ourselves, no matter how beautiful it is!

—Loren White, carver and sun dancer

Total trust,
surrender,
relinquishing control—
all this is only words.
Look into the night sky.
Tell me what you see.

—*The RuneCards*, Rune 25, The Unknowable

DAY
301

I accept and embrace my
limitations.
I accept and honor your
limitations.
Now we are free to
change and grow.

—*Relationships—A Compass for Conduct*, Rune 7, *Nauthiz*, Limitations

And when it finally arrives, welcome the day when the desire to remain the same is more painful than the risk of changing and growing.

DAY
302

O what am I that
I should not seem,
for the song's sake, a fool?

—William Butler Yeats

What if the physical passion between you is currently at low tide? If that is the case, open yourself to the intimacy of time spent together with no agenda, simply listening and speaking from your hearts. Passion evolves and grows as we grow, nourishing relationship in different ways, at different times of our lives. Like the phoenix, a passionate relationship endures the fire, and will rise again and again from what may look to the world like ashes.

DAY
304

—*Relationships—A Compass for Conduct*, Rune 15, *Teiwaz*, Passion

ere's a word to the wise: If you get into a resentful state of mind, simply by being in that state of mind you tune in by morphemic resonance with countless people who have been resentful in the past, including yourself. So you are actually influenced by your own past resentments and the resentments many other people have felt. You tune in to a generalized sense of resentment. These things are transpersonal, in the sense that they possess us.

—Matthew Fox and Rupert Sheldrake, *Natural Grace*

Do me one small favor,
my young friend—don't
take this world personally.

—Rev. Abraham Blum

DAY
307

Sometimes we mistake romance for intimacy, but romance is intimacy before you do the work, before you really get to know one another. For some of us, this Rune indicates that it is the time to stretch our understanding of intimacy beyond the romantic and the sexual, and get our feelings to touch in the ordinary moments of our life together.

Intimacy requires time. Receiving this Rune is a signal to value intimacy enough to make the time for it. Intimacy also requires patience, for true intimacy cannot be forced. Like sexuality, its energy will ebb and flow within your relationship. When intimacy is on the wane, know that it will return, and be patient.

—*Relationships—A Compass for Conduct*, Rune 8, *Inguz*, Intimacy

In the province of the
mind, there are no limits,
no boundaries. And yet,
if you are not careful,
you can be stuck with a
belief system.

—John Lilly

The need for restraint is unquestionable here. Drawing this Rune indicates that there may well be holdups and reasons to reconsider your plans carefully. Clearly there is work to be done on your self. So take it on with goodwill and show perseverance. This is a time to pay off old debts, to restore, if not harmony, at least balance. So mend, restore, redress: When fishermen can't go to sea, they repair nets.

—*The Book of Runes*, Rune 7, *Nauthiz*, Constraint

DAY 309

Follow the three Rs:
Respect for yourself,
Respect for others and
Responsibility for all
your actions.

—*Instructions for Life*

What you think you create
What you create you become
What you become you express
What you express you experience
What you experience you are
And since you are what you think …

Examine your limitations: You come from a certain background, you have lived your life in a particular way. As your limitations become clearer to you, you will begin to see that various notions you hold about yourself are not supported by the reality of your life … Through this process of limiting and specifying, your view of yourself will become clearer and more simple.

DAY
312

—*The RuneCards*

DAY
313

The best doctors
in the world
are
Doctor Diet,
Doctor Quiet,
and Doctor Merryman.

—Jonathan Swift (1667–1745)

When we quiet our mind and place our awareness in the keeping of Spirit, inner peace is sure to follow. Whatever your issue may be, whatever the challenge that faces you, *Kano* is saying, cease your struggling. Breathe out all tension and fear. Breathe in God's love and compassion. Breathe in the light of inner peace.

DAY
314

—*Relationships—A Compass for Conduct*, Rune 14, *Kano*, Inner Peace

Living in this chaotic environment, I've come to realize that unless you have a very close relationship with God, and unless you personally are living as exemplary a life as you can, then what you say to people isn't going to have much of an impact.

—John Cardinal O'Conner

Without perseverance, few intimate relationships could survive. For it is through perseverance that we create new attitudes and improve our skills for relating. Once you set your intention to change, you can begin to replace old, outmoded behavior with fresh and creative ways of relating to your partner.

DAY
316

—*Relationships—A Compass for Conduct*, Rune 13, *Jera*, Perseverance

NOVEMBER 12

A RELEASE EXERCISE
Light an eight-hour candle. Start with these words:

> *From the Highest possible Place*
> *And for the Greatest Possible Good …*

Write your name, and that of the particular matter, person or condition to be released. Then write:

> *I [your name] release all my fear around [name the person] and any harm they may do to me, my finances, my home or those I love. I release all my anger toward them and all my anxiety that they can hurt me in any way. And I place them in the light.*

Sign it. Read it out loud. Burn it. After eight hours, take what's left of the candle and place it in the garbage outside your house.

—Ellen Kelly, conversation

You may be dismayed at failing to
take right action. And yet rather
than dismay, what is called for here
is diligence. You may be required to
cultivate the soil once again, yet
through correct preparation, growth
is assured.

—*The Book of Runes*, Rune 16, *Berkana* Reversed, Growth

My understanding of the Great Pumpkin's time schedule goes something like this: Don't fret if you think something should be coming about; just do what you can, as best you can, and if you can't, then don't worry; it will all fall into place in a way we can never fathom at the time.

—Jeanne Blum, e-mail, November 14, 2000 C.E.

I cherish you now. I will cherish you for as long as our lives entwine. In faith I renew my commitment to you every day.

DAY
320

—*Relationships—A Compass for Conduct*, Rune 2, *Gebo*, Commitment

Here's the good news: If you can change your own programming—your unconscious, automatic responses—the energy of the Relationship will definitely change. Only one partner needs to cross the divide. This could entail abandoning a form of behavior that doesn't serve you anymore. Or it might simply mean choosing to take better care of yourself.

—*Relationships—A Compass for Conduct*, Rune 5, *Uruz*, Support

No person made a greater
mistake than the one who
did nothing because he
could only do a little.

—Edmund Burke

At the heart of openness is the need for acceptance—acceptance of ourselves, acceptance of others, and acceptance of the right of all God's creatures to be in the world. Once there is openness and acceptance, self-change becomes a real possibility. We were all born open to life—and open to change. Now is the time to reclaim our birthright.

—*The Serenity Runes*, Envoi

Look at it this way: Each time you face the issue of Trust, you are being asked to grow. When you push through your fears and trust your feelings, you do grow—and Trust grows in you.

DAY
324

Receiving this Rune, you are encouraged to take the first step, to reclaim the lost Trust you once cherished and thrived upon. We are born to live our lives in Trust. Let no one tell you differently.

—*The Healing Runes*, Rune 2, Trust

There is hardly a better time to interrupt an old pattern than when you are under pressure and the stress is mounting.

Basically, says Iyanla Vanzant, most of us come from "a belief in lack." Here's how she put it on *The Oprah Winfrey Show* that aired in Hawaii on July 24, 1998:

> *If you want it*
> *You ain't got it*
> *If you ain't got it*
> *You can't give it*
> *If you can't give it*
> *You can't receive it*
> *And if you can't receive it, you're*
> *going to be left wanting it, from which*
> *it follows that you've got a problem.*

DAY
327

In the context of relationship, *Dagaz* is the light of shared purpose that gives deeper meaning to life. Behind such purpose lies vision, and from it comes service.

—*Relationships—A Compass for Conduct*, Rune 22, *Dagaz*, Purpose

What you and I are doing now, together, is like sitting practice or walking meditation. Listening in this way, I know that I will hear you when you speak. Even though I may have a solution when you whistle the first few bars, part of that solution is hearing you out with patience and concern. And just as precious, I know that when I need to speak to you, you will most certainly hear me. Where I come from, that's called a conversation. Relationships thrive on it.

DAY
328

—Maui, Christmas 1997

DAY
329

Too often we deny ourselves the healing power of pleasure in our need to get ahead in the world. We forgo the pleasure of walking in the garden, playing with a child, the pleasure of good company—all of which can be healing for the soul. We become so caught up in getting and spending, that we deny ourselves the restorative power of simply being.

—*Relationships—A Compass for Conduct*, Rune 15, *Teiwaz*, Passion

There are three things a woman needs to know from her man: That she is seen. That she is cared for. That she is loved. Along with "seen" goes "heard." While "cared for" is far wider than paying the bills. As for "loved," the ways of demonstrating it are difficult to count, yet easy to recognize.

In disagreements with loved ones, deal only with the current situation. Don't bring up the past. All too often, the past is a virus on the hard drive of relationship.

DAY
331

As we start to make contact with our Knowing Selves, we will begin to hear messages of profound beauty and true usefulness. For like snowflakes and fingerprints, each of our oracular signatures is a one-of-a-kind aspect of Creation addressing its own.

—*The Book of Runes*

DAY
333

To know the mind of God, listen to your heart.

—Melody Beattie, *The Lessons of Love*

Eight gifts that do not cost a cent:

1. The Gift of Listening
2. The Gift of Affection
3. The Gift of Laughter
4. The Gift of a Written Note
5. The Gift of a Compliment
6. The Gift of a Kindness
7. The Gift of Solitude
8. The Gift of a Cheerful Disposition

DAY
334

—Received over the internet

DAY
335

The Viking Runes are a mirror for the magic of our Knowing Selves. In time, as you become skilled in their use, you can lay the Runes aside and permit the knowing to arise unfiltered, just as some dowsers use only their bare hands to find water.

—*The Book of Runes*

The Unknowable represents the path of karma—the sum total of your actions and their consequences, the lessons that are yours for this lifetime. And yet this Rune teaches that the very debts of old karma shift and evolve as you shift and evolve. Nothing is predestined: What beckons is the creative power of the unknown.

DAY
336

Whenever you draw The Blank Rune, take heart: Know that the work of self-change is progressing in your life.

—*The Book of Runes*, Rune 25, The Blank Rune

Words to be written on the blackboard of the
heart as often as required to dissolve anger and
turn aside harsh feelings:

I will speak to you only as someone I love.
I will speak to you only as someone I love.
I will speak to you only as someone I love.
I will speak to you only as someone I love.
I will speak to you only as someone I love.

Followers of Tao use patterns when planning. They observe the ways of nature, perceive the invisible lines of destiny. They imagine a pattern for their entire lives and in this way they ensure overall success … When unpredictable things happen, those who follow Tao are also skilled at improvisation. If circumstances deny them, they improvise; that is their ultimate art.

—Tao: Daily Meditations

We are the salt of the earth.
We are the light of the world.

When you are sorely pressed, turn
within and find once more the peace
That passes understanding.

—*Relationships—A Compass for Conduct*, Rune 14, *Kano*, Inner Peace

Timor mortis conturbat me ...
Latin, meaning, "The fear of
death churns me up." So what is
to be done? Wade into it, meet it
before it comes, embrace it, and
know death as friend and wise
counselor. True, this may take
some doing; yet refusing to do it
will be my undoing.

DAY
341

You can forgive someone, accept who they are, and still choose to leave the relationship. Interests may pull you in different directions, until one day you look up and realize you're no longer on the same road. Sometimes the only way to renew your relationship with yourself is by leaving.

—*Relationships—A Compass for Conduct*, Rune 17, *Ehwaz*, Renewal

In her lovely book *The Mysterious Spiral: Journey of the Soul*, Jill Purce writes: "Because any description of the Absolute must be limited, we are able to reveal it only by using symbols, which cut directly through all the layers and windings of our consciousness."

Indeed. That is one of the primary functions of the Runes.

DAY
343

In receiving this Rune, it is good to consider the end of our own allotted time, to rehearse and plan as we would plan for any significant event. God willing, you will die at home, free of pain, surrounded by those you love, with sufficient time to say thank yous and farewells. Perhaps this is the letting go for which all the others are merely practice.

—*Relationships—A Compass for Conduct*, Rune 6, *Perth*, Letting Go

No one can persuade another
to change. Each of us guards a
gate of change that can only be
opened from the inside. There
is no way we can open the gate
of another, either by emotional
appeal or by argument.

—Marilyn Ferguson

DAY
345

Make me honest enough to admit all my shortcomings; smart enough to accept praise without becoming arrogant; tall enough to tower above deceit; strong enough to welcome criticism; compassionate enough to understand human frailties; wise enough to recognize my own mistakes; humble enough to appreciate greatness in others; staunch enough to stand by my friends; human enough to be thoughtful of my neighbor; and righteous enough to be devoted to the love of God.

—Internet wisdom

Blank is the end, blank the beginning. This is the Rune of total trust and should be taken as exciting evidence of your most immediate contact with your own true destiny which, time and again, rises like the phoenix from the ashes of what we call fate.

The appearance of this Rune can portend a death. However that death is usually symbolic and may relate to any part of your life as you are living it now. *Relinquishing control is the ultimate challenge for the Spiritual Warrior.*

—*The Book of Runes*, Rune 25, The Blank Rune

Forgive, do not fear, do not anticipate attack, focus all your energy in the here and now of your body and mind. Be at peace. Be still. And in the stillness and peace, let your seeing and your listening come from Total Self, which is the unencumbered will of God. And in the free form of Creation you will know the moves to make.

—*A Course in Miracles*

There is a prayer, known as the *Gayatri*, that embodies the spirit of the Rune of Wholeness. Address the sun in this fashion:

> *You who are the source of all power,*
> *Whose rays illuminate the world,*
> *Illuminate also my heart*
> *So that it too can do Your work.*

DAY
348

While reciting the *Gayatri*, visualize the sun's rays streaming forth into the world, entering your heart, then streaming out from your heart's center and back into the world. This is a powerful and life-enhancing prayer.

— *The Book of Runes*, Rune 24, *Sowelu*, Wholeness

You might say the Runes are just another way of calling home.

—Talk with Fr. Bede Griffiths, Tamil Nadu, India 1986

A crisis, a difficult passage—even if brief—is at hand. Consideration and deliberation are called for now. Ask yourself whether you possess the virtues of seriousness, sincerity, and emptiness; to possess them is to have tranquillity, which is the ground for patience, clarity and perseverance.

DAY
350

—*The Book of Runes*, Rune 12, *Wunjo* Reversed, Joy

DAY
351

Praise Winter.
  Gather snowdrops.
Listen for your name
   on the chill wind
   and bless the seeds
    waiting in the darkness
for the call of Spring.

—*The RuneCards*, Rune 23, *Isa*, Standstill

There was something, undefined
and complete, coming into existence
before Heaven and Earth. How still
it was and formless, standing alone
and undergoing no change, reaching
everywhere and in no danger of
being exhausted. It may be regarded
as the Mother of all things.

—Lao-tzu, *Tao Te Ching*

DAY
353

This Rune urges vigilance and continual mindfulness, especially in times of good fortune, for it is then that you are likely to collapse yourself into your success on the one hand, or behave recklessly on the other. Enjoy your good fortune and remember to share it: The mark of the well-nourished self is the ability and willingness to nourish others.

—*The Book of Runes*, Rune 11, *Fehu*, Possessions

So how does an Oracle work?
If you are facing northeast, and
the answer happens to lie in the
southwest, it is of considerable
use to have a friend who takes
your arm and turns you in the
direction where you need to look.
The Runes are such a friend.

DAY
354

DAY
355

Dear God,
I pray, keep me mindful
of your presence in the objects, events
and persons of ordinary life, since I know
*   it's true*
that you both hide and reveal yourself
in the ordinary.

Remember, you cannot abandon
what you do not know.
To go beyond yourself, you must
know yourself.

—Sri Nisargadatta Maharaj

DAY
357

May the strength of God pilot us.
May the power of God preserve us.
May the wisdom of God instruct us.
May the hand of God protect us.
May the way of God direct us.
May the shield of God defend us.

—Attributed to St. Patrick

Undertake your passage
   in trust and innocence,
for such is the Warrior Way.
And at the end,
   send heavenward
      the burning arrows
of your perfect faith.

—*The RuneCards*, Rune 15, *Teiwaz*, The Warrior

I have prayed for what I needed
Giving thanks for what I had
My soul and heart are seeded
Thoughts of harvest make me glad
We are born of wind and water
We are promised to the sky

I have loved you
Since I found you
I will love you 'til I die

I am one with all creatures
And none is ever lost
But only restored to me
Having never left me at all.
For what is Eternal
Cannot be separated from its
Source.

—*The Book of Runes*

*O Divine Master, grant that
I may not so much seek
To be consoled as to console,
To be understood as to understand,
To be loved as to love.
For it is in giving that we receive.
It is in pardoning that we are pardoned.
It is in dying that we are born to eternal life.*

—St. Francis of Assisi

ractice the art of doing without doing: Aim yourself truly and then maintain your aim without manipulative effort. Meditate on Christ's words: I can of mine own self do nothing (John 5:30). For by our own power we do nothing: even in loving, it is Love that loves through us. This way of thinking and being integrates new energies and permits you to flow into wholeness, which is the ultimate goal of the Spiritual Warrior.

DAY
362

—*The Book of Runes*, Rune 24, *Sowelu*, Wholeness

If mine were the last turn,
And the dice lay charmed
  in the cup,
I would seek to change nothing.

The ability and willingness to compromise is
evidence of your intention to cherish and
nourish one another. Evidence that you love
your neighbor as you love yourself. When
such is the case, regardless of the nature of the
situation, you will always be able to work
things out, and you will honor one another
and the relationship through your skills in the
art of compromise.

DAY
364

—*Relationships—A Compass for Conduct*, Rune 21, *Thurisaz*, Compromise

As midnight approaches, it is Lady Julian of Norwich who recalls us to peace of heart:

"All shall be well, and all shall be well, and all manner of things shall be well."

Kano Reversed calls for giving up gladly the old and being prepared to live for a time empty... and carries the warning not to be seduced by the momentum of old ways while waiting for the new to become illuminated in their proper time.

—*The Book of Runes*, Rune 14, *Kano* Reversed, Opening

Rune Names

		BOOK OF RUNES	HEALING RUNES	RELATIONSHIP RUNES	GERMANIC NAME
1	ᛗ	The Self	Innocence	Loving Kindness	*Mannaz*
2	ᚷ	Partnership	Trust	Commitment	*Gebo*
3	ᚠ	Signals	Guilt	Communication	*Ansuz*
4	ᛜ	Separation	Grief	Home and Family	*Othila*
5	ᚢ	Strength	Gratitude	Support	*Uruz*
6	ᛈ	Initiation	Love	Letting Go	*Perth*
7	ᚾ	Constraint	Shame	Limitations	*Nauthiz*
8	ᛝ	Fertility	Faith	Intimacy	*Inguz*
9	ᛇ	Defense	Denial	Respect	*Eihwaz*
10	ᛉ	Protection	Boundaries	Mutual Trust	*Algiz*
11	ᚨ	Possessions	Honesty	Abundance	*Fehu*
12	ᚹ	Joy	Serenity	Celebration	*Wunjo*
13	ᛃ	Harvest	Patience	Perseverance	*Jera*

		BOOK OF RUNES	HEALING RUNES	RELATIONSHIP RUNES	GERMANIC NAME
14	ᚲ	Opening	Acceptance	Inner Peace	*Kano*
15	↑	Warrior	Courage	Passion	*Teiwaz*
16	ᛒ	Growth	Prayer	Right Action	*Berkana*
17	ᛗ	Movement	Forgiveness	Renewal	*Ehwaz*
18	ᚦ	Flow	Humor	Change	*Laguz*
19	ᚺ	Disruption	Anger	Challenges	*Hagalaz*
20	ᚱ	Journey	Surrender	Harmony	*Raido*
21	ᚦ	Gateway	Wisdom	Compromise	*Thurisaz*
22	ᛉ	Breakthrough	Hope	Purpose	*Dagaz*
23	ᛁ	Standstill	Fear	Reflection	*Isa*
24	ᛋ	Wholeness	Compassion	Healing	*Sowelu*
25		Unknowable	The Divine	The Mystery	

Acknowledgments

Bibliographical details of the excerpts, other than those by Ralph H. Blum, in this book are given below, with copyright notices and permissions indicated where appropriate. Every effort has been made to acknowledge the copyright owner of the material used. If any acknowledgment has been inadvertently omitted, the copyright owner is invited to contact the author care of Connections Book Publishing at the address given at the front of this book.

Page 22: Rainer Maria Rilke *The Best of Rilke*, University Press of New England.

Pages 55, 134, 316: Matthew Fox and Rupert Sheldrake, *Natural Grace*, Bloomsbury.

Pages 74 and 158: A portion of *A Course in Miracles*® copyright © 1975, 1992, 1996, reprinted by permission of the Foundation for *A Course in Miracles*, Inc.® (www.facim.org). All rights reserved. *A Course in Miracles*® is a registered trademark of the *Foundation for A Course in Miracles*®.

Page 173: Joel S. Goldsmith *The Altitude of Prayer*, Acropolis Books, Inc.

Page 202: Thanks to Ian Anderson for permission to reproduce *Broadsword* by Jethro Tull.

Page 227: Kahlil Gibran *The Prophet*, Wordsworth Editions.

Page 250: Marianne Williamson *A Return to Love*, copyright © 1992 by Marianne Williamson, reprinted by permission of HarperCollins Publishers Inc.

Page 299: From *The Tibetan Book of the Dead* copyright © 1975 by Francesca Fremantle and Chögyam Trungpa. Reprinted by arrangement with Shambhala Publications, Inc., Boston, www.shambhala.com.

Page 344: Melody Beattie *Lessons of Love*, copyright © 1994 by Melody Beattie, reprinted by permission of HarperCollins Publishers, Inc.

Page 353: Jill Purce *The Mysterious Spiral*, Thames and Hudson.

Other titles by Ralph H. Blum

The Book of Runes Tenth Anniversary Edition,
    St. Martin's Press, 1993.
Rune Play, St. Martin's Press, 1985.
The RuneCards, St. Martin's Press, 1989.
The Healing Runes (with Susan Loughan),
    St. Martin's Press, 1995.
The Serenity Runes (with Susan Loughan and
    Bronwyn E. Jones), St. Martin's Press, 1998.
Relationships—A Compass for Conduct (with Jeanne Blum),
    St. Martin's Press, 2002.

The RuneWorks

The RuneWorks was established in 1983 as a resource for people working with the Viking Runes. Now, we at the RuneWorks are especially interested in hearing of your experiences with the Runes. Please feel encouraged to write to us at The RuneWorks:

P.O. Box 1193
Idyllwild
CA 92549
USA

Author's acknowledgments

I should like to thank the entire fellowship at Eddison Sadd, and especially to:

Nick Eddison for suggesting that I draw from the oracular midden a mix of thoughts, ideas, and compass bearings that now make up this book.

Ian Jackson for his thoughtful suggestions on the manuscript, and for keeping the snaffle and martingale tight and in place.

Elaine Partington for her impeccable designing ways.

Nicola Hodgson for keeping calm in the face of constant changes.

Liz Wheeler, who backed up and eagle-eyed the lot, assisted by Michele Turney and Eleanor Van Zandt.

Brazzle Atkins, the venerable Mac Designer on our little book.

Karyn Claridge and Charles James for handling the production with such esprit de corps.

Jeanne Elizabeth Blum, who edited and proofread in the early rounds, so we could prevail.

Bronwyn Jones, whose dedication and editing panache were essential.